They walked toward the lagoon, arm in arm

"I've enjoyed your company very much," Rick said, echoing her own thoughts.

There was something electrifying between them, and Dale's mind warned her to be on her guard. "I think we'd better go inside."

She turned from him, and in her haste, tripped, but his arms cushioned her fall. Cradling her against him, he took possession of her parted lips. She responded to his sensual demand wildly, but only for a moment. His contempt that night of the storm had cut too deep, and then there was Melissa Arnell. "Let me go, Rick," she heard herself say, and he released her at once.

"You'd better go into the house," he said tersely, and with a hint of hateful mockery he added, "Take care this time that you don't trip and fall, because I shan't be there to pick you up."

YVONNE WHITTAL
is also the author of these

Harlequin Presents

and these

Harlequin Romances

Many of these books are available at your local bookseller.

For a free catalog listing all titles currently available, send your
name and address to:

HARLEQUIN READER SERVICE
1440 South Priest Drive, Tempe, AZ 85281
Canadian address: Stratford, Ontario N5A 6W2

YVONNE WHITTAL

dark heritage

Harlequin Books

TORONTO • NEW YORK • LONDON
AMSTERDAM • PARIS • SYDNEY • HAMBURG
STOCKHOLM • ATHENS • TOKYO • MILAN

Harlequin Presents first edition September 1983
ISBN 0-373-10630-0

Original hardcover edition published in 1983
by Mills & Boon Limited

CHAPTER ONE

THE shady summerhouse in the spacious grounds of St Stephen's Academy for Girls was out of bounds, and Dale Palmer looked up with a guilty start when someone entered it unexpectedly, but she was relieved when she found herself staring up into Sister Teresa's tranquil face.

'When you were neither in your room nor in the library, I knew I would find you here,' the nun smiled, her glance shifting to the book in Dale's lap. 'What are you reading?'

'*The Art and Architecture of the Renaissance,*' Dale replied, closing the book so that Sister Teresa could see the cover.

'That's rather heavy reading, isn't it?'

'I find it very interesting.'

Sister Teresa surveyed the small, slim girl who sat curled up on the wooden bench, and her brown eyes softened. In her floral cotton frock and white sandals Dale looked like a fifteen-year-old instead of a girl of nineteen who was about to take her matriculation examinations.

'Why don't you study art next year instead of enrolling for a secretarial course?' Sister Teresa questioned Dale, not for the first time, but Dale shook her head firmly.

'Art is my hobby, and I want it to remain that way.'

Sister Teresa sighed and clasped her hands together in a gesture of resignation, then a slight frown creased her brow as she looked down on the bowed head before her. 'Mr Crawford, your attorney, is here to see you.'

Dale's head shot up, and at that moment her blue eyes looked almost too large for her small, pointed face. 'My attorney?'

'That's what I'm told,' Sister Teresa confirmed briskly. 'He is with Mother Superior in her office, and I'm to take you there at once.'

St Stephen's Academy for Girls was a school of repute in Durban, but it had become more than simply a school to Dale Palmer. It had been her home since the age of six, and the nuns, Sister Teresa in particular, had taken the place of her family. Ivan and Celeste Palmer had spent their lives travelling the world, and an occasional postcard had at times been the only communication Dale had received. Their visits had been rare and brief, and she could count on one hand the holidays she had actually spent at home. She had been notified two weeks ago of the death of her parents in an accident which had occurred during a chartered flight across the Alps in Europe, and although the news had come as a shock, Dale had not found it unduly distressing. Now, quite suddenly, she was told that she possessed such a thing as an attorney, and the knowledge was more than a little unnerving.

'Sister Teresa, I——'

'Come, child,' the nun interrupted with an encouraging smile. 'I'm certain you have no reason at all to be afraid.'

Dale followed Sister Teresa from the summerhouse on that warm October afternoon, and beyond the privet hedge she could detect the laughter of the hostel girls enjoying the break before the late afternoon study period. Their laughter had never troubled her before, but at that moment it almost seemed to mock her as she followed Sister Teresa into the grey stone building. The light touch of a hand on Dale's arm made her pause in her stride as they approached the Mother Superior's quarters, and she glanced at the nun beside her, her nervousness clearly visible in the wide blue eyes.

'You'd better give me that book,' Sister Teresa warned gently. 'It wouldn't do for Mother Superior to know you've been reading about the Renaissance instead of studying your physical science.'

'I know my science,' Dale protested, handing over the book and watching it disappear smartly beneath Sister Teresa's white habit.

'I know that, child,' the nun smiled, her dark eyes twinkling with mischief, 'but Mother Superior doesn't!'

An answering smile plucked at the corners of Dale's full, sensitive mouth, and a few moments later Sister Teresa was ushering her into Mother Superior's office. Nervous tension settled like a cloak about Dale. She heard Sister Teresa murmur something encouraging, then she departed silently and left Dale alone to face this new crisis in her young life.

The priory office was cool and sparsely furnished, but Dale was well acquainted with this room, *and* the woman in the white garb who turned to face her.

'Come in, Dale,' Mother Superior coaxed her away from the door. 'This is Mr Crawford. He was your father's legal adviser, and he is now going to serve you in that same capacity.'

Dale's bewildered glance settled on the man who had ceased his conversation with Mother Superior the moment Dale had entered the room. He was tall and lean, with dark hair cropped close to his proud head, and equally dark, penetrating eyes observed her from beneath dark, sardonically arched brows. His high-bridged nose was straight above the thin, stern mouth, and his deeply tanned skin seemed to stretch too tightly from his cheekbones down to his firm, jutting jaw. He looked imposing and formidable, and there hovered about him an undeniable air of authority as he turned to address the Mother Superior.

'I wonder if you would permit me to speak to her alone,' he said, and his voice was pleasantly deep and well-modulated.

'I shall be in the next room if you should need me,' Mother Superior nodded amiably. 'Simply press that button on my desk.'

She left the room and closed the interleading door quietly behind her, leaving Dale alone with this man who was observing her much as she imagined one would observe an object under a microscope in the laboratory. Plain and painfully thin, with mousy-coloured hair braided into a single plait that hung down her back, Dale began to feel she was twice as unattractive. She was accustomed to the often cruel mockery of her classmates, and could deal with it, but this man's silent appraisal unnerved her. His immobile features gave her no indication as to what he was thinking, and she withdrew from him mentally as a measure of self-defence.

'Won't you sit down, Dale?' He gestured towards the wooden upright chair beside her, and, when she was seated, he pulled a chair closer for himself and lowered his lean length on to it. 'How much do you know of your father's business?'

'I know he was an importer of engineering products,' she answered him truthfully, sitting rigidly erect on the edge of her chair with her hands clasped nervously in her lap.

'Is that all you know?' he questioned, flicking an imaginary speck of dust off the sleeve of his dark, immaculately tailored suit.

'My parents travelled extensively because of the nature of my father's work,' she added, wondering what all these questions were leading up to, and the attorney did not waste time in enlightening her.

'Your father has left you a very wealthy young woman, and as one of the main shareholders you could one day take charge as a director of the company, if you wish.' His compelling eyes held hers captive while she silently digested this astonishing information, but he followed it up with something which disturbed her even more. 'Until you're twenty-one, however, I am to be your legal adviser and guardian.'

'You—You're to be my guardian?' she stammered, sinking her small teeth nervously into her quivering lip to steady it.

'That's right.' He flicked a glance at her hands laced so tightly in her lap that her knuckles shone white through the pale skin. 'I believe you've chosen to go to a secretarial college for a year.'

Y—Yes,' she croaked nervously.

'Have you no interest in a career which involves the economics of business?'

'No,' she shook her head adamantly, her mind firmly set on attending the secretarial college.

'Very well, then.' He rose to his feet, and Dale felt compelled to do the same, but she found herself totally dwarfed by this man's length. 'You may rest assured that I shall attend to the business side of your inheritance to the best of my ability.'

The finality in his voice seemed to bring the discussion to an end and, stepping a pace away from him, she asked timidly, 'May—May I go now?'

'Not yet.' He smiled for the first time, a smile that simply curved his lips, but which never quite reached his dark, probing eyes. 'You'll be taking your final exams shortly. As soon as you're allowed out for the holidays you'll be collected and taken to my home in Westville.'

Alarm shot through her, and caught at her throat like the tightening of a noose. 'I would rather remain here at St Stephen's.'

'That may be so, but once you've taken your finals you will no longer be a scholar at this Academy, and you're old enough to know that the nuns cannot continue providing a home for you indefinitely,' he argued impatiently, then his brows rose in a decidedly mocking manner above his eyes. 'Unless, of course, you intend taking your vows to become one of them?'

'No, I—I don't, but——'

'In that case you must trust me to decide what's best for you in the future,' he cut short her faltering protest.

'I suppose so,' Dale agreed miserably.

'Is there perhaps anything you require before I leave? Money, for instance?'

A strong hand with long, well-tapered fingers slid into the inside pocket of his jacket as if to wip out his cheque book and pen, and her reply tumbled hastily from her lips. 'I don't need anything, thank you.'

'If you should need anything, then I trust you'll contact me at once.' His hand emerged from his pocket, but, instead of a cheque book, he held a small white card between his fingers. 'You will find my home and office telephone numbers on that card.'

'Thank you,' she murmured politely, accepting the card from him with a hand that trembled slightly.

He waited, almost as if he expected her to study the card, then he swung away from her abruptly and pressed the button on the desk. The interleading door opened almost at once, and Mother Superior's calm countenance eased away some of the tension in Dale's taut body.

'I would like to thank you for these few minutes alone with Dale,' the attorney said, using Dale's name once again with an ease which surprised her.

The Mother Superior's eyes were filled with concern as she glanced at Dale. 'Do you understand and accept everything, my child?'

'Yes, Mother,' Dale whispered an affirmative reply

despite the confusion that still reigned within her.
'May I go now?'

'You may go,' Mother Superior nodded, and Dale
was surprised to discover that her legs were shaking as
she walked out of the office.

Alone in the small room which she was privileged
not to have to share with anyone, she tried to
assimilate the news which the attorney had just
imparted to her. She had known very little about her
parents other than that her father had been kind,
whereas her beautiful mother had made no secret of
the fact that she disliked her 'ugly duckling' daughter.
'Put her in a convent. The nuns will look after her,'
Celeste had said when it was time for Dale to start
school, and Ivan Palmer had not argued away his
wife's cruel rejection of their child.

Dale, as young as she had been at that time, had
sensed that she was unwanted, and as the years passed
she became a withdrawn young woman who preferred
sketching, or reading to associating with the other girls
in the Academy. They inevitably passed cruel remarks
concerning her behaviour and her plainness, and
succeeded in heightening that feeling of being
unwanted. Sister Teresa was Dale's only true friend
and confidant and, owing to the fact that she had had
to spend so many holidays at the Academy while the
other girls had gone to their various homes, Dale
enjoyed a few privileges which were denied to the
others. She had a room to herself, even though it was
no larger than the Academy's pantry, she had access to
the library any time of the day she wished, and she
could visit the private chapel within the grounds
whenever she felt the need to do so.

Dale stared at the card she was twisting agitatedly
between her fingers, and read for the first time the
words printed on it. *R. J. Crawford, Attorney.* His
home and office telephone numbers followed, but her

fingers were shaking so much that she could barely
read then. He had mentioned money, but all the money
in the world could not make up for the years of
knowing that she had been unwanted. She had been
reared by servants until it was time for her to go to
school, and then she had been passed on to the nuns
like an obnoxious parcel. Her future had been placed
in their hands, and now she found herself in the slim-
fingered hands of *R. J. Crawford, Attorney*. He was to
be her guardian and legal adviser until she came of
age, and she would once again become an unwanted
burden.

A light tap on the door made Dale look up to see
Sister Teresa entering her room, and the tender smile
in those dark eyes warmed Dale's heart.

'I waited for you in the summerhouse,' she said,
'but when you didn't come I knew you'd be here in
your room.'

'I had a lot to think about,' Dale explained lamely
when Sister Teresa sat down beside her on the bed,
her weight making the bed springs creak.

'What did Mr Crawford have to tell you?'

'My parents left me a lot of money,' Dale replied,
her expression distasteful. 'And he's to be my legal
adviser and guardian until I turn twenty-one.'

'What's so terrible about that?'

'I don't want their money!' Dale cried in distress.
'And I don't need a guardian!'

A slim white hand gripped her arm. 'You can't stay
here for ever, Dale, and I'm sure Mr Crawford will
see to it that you're well taken care of.' She paused
momentarily, characteristically letting her words sink
into Dale's mind before she continued speaking. 'As
for your inheritance, child, accept it for what it's
worth—a legacy left to you by your parents with
which you can further your career.'

'Why should I accept their money when——'

'Don't say it, child,' Sister Teresa interrupted hastily. 'Don't torture yourself with the things you don't understand, and perhaps never will understand.'

'I know they didn't want me,' Dale argued, her eyes brimming with unshed tears. 'My mother was so beautiful, and I know she couldn't stand having a plain, unattractive daughter like me.'

'A few unkind words when one is at a tender age can prey on the mind and distort one's vision when confronted with a mirror so that one sees only what one believes is there,' Sister Teresa spoke in gentle earnest. 'Beauty, dear child, comes mostly from within, and in that you surpass your mother. You have great depths, and a wonderful capacity to love. Cling to that thought, and don't allow bitterness to soil your heart and twist your mind until you're blind to everything else.'

That evening, after dinner, Dale sought the peace and solitude of the chapel, and she remained there for almost an hour before she felt calm enough to return to her room and go to bed.

Sister Teresa was standing beside Dale on the steps of St Stephen's when a white Mercedes drove through the gates and came up the long drive towards them. A little more than six weeks ago Dale had met the attorney for the first time, she had taken her final exams in the interim, and now he was taking her away from those she loved to go and live with him at his home. She glanced at the nun in her white garb standing beside her, and she bit her trembling lip to steady it. She had said goodbye to everyone else without a tear, and she was not going to cry now when she had to say farewell to Sister Teresa.

The tyres of the Mercedes crunched on the gravel as it slid to a halt beside the steps, and Dale watched with a calmness she was far from experiencing as Mr

Crawford, the attorney, uncoiled his lean length from the interior of the car to come up the steps towards them. He was wearing a dark grey suit on this occasion, but looked no less intimidating than on the first occasion they had met.

Dale introduced him to Sister Teresa, and they shook hands briefly, then he glanced down at the battered suitcase and small box of books that stood on the marble step at Dale's feet. She had considered his lean features immobile, but on this occasion his black brows rose in sharp surprise.

'Is this all?' he asked in his deep, somewhat abrupt voice as he gestured towards her meagre possessions.

'Yes, Mr Crawford,' she replied nervously, and she saw his stern mouth tighten as he picked up her belongings, and carried them down the steps to his car.

Dale and Sister Teresa followed in silence, but when he had slammed down the lid of the trunk and locked it, Sister Teresa asked with some concern, 'You will take good care of Dale, won't you, Mr Crawford?'

He smiled briefly that mirthless smile Dale had witnessed once before. 'You have my word on that.'

'God bless you,' Sister Teresa replied.

The attorney was impatient to leave, Dale could sense it in his manner, and she felt sick as she realised the time had come to say farewell to the one woman who had been mother, friend, and spiritual adviser through all the years of her childhood.

'I shan't say goodbye,' she said, in a rush to get the words past the rising lump in her throat and, gripping the hands Sister Teresa extended towards her, she added: 'I'll come and visit you whenever I can, Sister Teresa.'

'Bless you, child,' the nun smiled, but there was a sadness in her eyes that almost sent Dale rushing headlong into her arms. 'I shall look forward to your visits.'

A hand touched Dale's shoulder lightly, a visible indication that it was time to leave and, turning from Sister Teresa, she got into the Mercedes. They were half way down the long drive towards the tall iron gates when she turned in her seat to glance back at the solitary figure in white on the marble steps and, opening the window, she waved for the last time. Sister Teresa's hand rose in swift response, and moments later she was hidden from view as the attorney edged his car into the traffic on that hot, humid afternoon on the last day of November.

Dale sat with her hands folded primly in her lap during the drive out to his home in Westville. Her throat felt tight, and there was a sting behind her eyelids, but she was determined not to cry. It was not the end of the world, but a new beginning, Sister Teresa had said only recently, and she would hold fast to that thought.

The attorney did not attempt to make conversation, and neither did Dale, but she observed him unobtrusively while he concentrated on the heavy late afternoon traffic. He was not a young man, but neither was he old, and she found herself judging his age somewhere in the region of thirty-five. There were laughter lines about his eyes, although she could not imagine this stern man ever doing such a thing, and deep grooves ran almost from his nose to his mouth. She wondered suddenly why her father had chosen this man to be her guardian. It was futile attempting to unravel the workings of her parents' minds; she knew too little about them to even try, and, thrusting her queries from her mind, she made the resolution to live each day as it came.

The attorney's home was not at all what she had imagined. It was a magnificent two-storied building surrounded by green lawns, and luscious trees and shrubs. Through the trees to the right of the house, she glimpsed some tall fencing which surrounded what looked like a tennis court, and her interest quickened. She enjoyed a game of tennis, and she hoped she would have the opportunity to indulge in this activity.

Mr Crawford parked his Mercedes beneath a pergola where a scarlet bougainvillaea provided sufficient shade and, not waiting for him to open the door for her, she slipped out of the car at the same time as he. She walked round to the trunk to stand about nervously while he removed her possessions from the boot, and her nerves reacted violently to the sound of the lid being slammed down.

'Mr Crawford, I——' She paused awkwardly, and he halted in the act of picking up her things to glance down at her questioningly. His unfathomable eyes unnerved her, but she knew she could no longer delay the burning query which had been hovering on the fringe of her mind for weeks. 'Didn't your wife object to having me in your home?'

That stern mouth twitched with the merest hint of amusement. 'I'm not married.'

'Oh!' she said, feeling foolish, but oddly relieved.

'I live here with my mother, and she's been looking forward tremendously to having you.' His compelling eyes probed hers mockingly. 'Does that set your mind at rest?'

'I'm sorry,' she managed, biting down hard on her quivering lip, and looking down at the brown, well-worn leather sandals on her feet when she could no longer sustain his glance. 'It's just that I—I would hate to be an inconvenience to anyone.'

'Let's get one thing straight before we go in,' he said in a clipped voice, and, clutching her hands nervously behind her back, she raised her wide blue eyes to his once more. 'I like my comforts, as you can see, and I like my home run on well-oiled wheels. If I'd thought that your coming here would disrupt my life in any way, then I would never have suggested it. Do I make myself clear?'

Dale shrank inwardly as she stared up at this tall, lean man before her. 'Yes, Mr Crawford.'

'And there's one other thing,' he added harshly, gripping her box of books under one arm and picking up her suitcase. 'My name is Rick. If we're going to live together in the same house for the next few years, then I suggest you use it.'

'Yes, Mr—Rick,' she stumbled nervously over his name, and her cheeks went pink with embarrassment, but he had turned away from her with a mixture of boredom and impatience on his face.

'Come on,' he barked abruptly. 'We've kept my mother waiting long enough.'

Dale followed him into the house with its spacious hall, its chandeliers and expensive furnishings. She felt nervous and ill at ease, but her nervousness vanished the moment Brenda Crawford stepped into the hall to meet them. She was obviously a woman in her mid-sixties, and she was tall and slender like her son. The whiteness against her temples was like silver wings in her otherwise dark hair, and dark brown eyes smiled down at Dale with a warmth that melted some of the icy awkwardness of their first meeting.

'Dale, my dear, I'm so happy to meet you at last!' A delicately feminine perfume lingered about her as she embraced Dale's small, thin figure, then she linked her arm through Dale's and drew her towards the carpeted stairs. 'Come, let me show you up to your room, then we can all have some tea.' Glancing briefly over her shoulder, she said to her son, 'Bring the child's things up with you, Rick.'

'I'm right behind you, Mother,' he sighed tolerantly.

'I've given you a room with your own private bathroom, and I sincerely hope you'll be very happy here with us,' Brenda Crawford chatted as they ascended the stairs and followed the passage down towards the left.

'That's very kind of you, Mrs Crawford,' Dale murmured, acutely conscious of the man who was following them in silence.

'Here we are,' Brenda said at last, opening a door and standing aside for Dale to precede her into the room.

The room she was to occupy was a fairy-tale of deep rose-pink and white. Dale had never seen anything so lovely before, and she was totally speechless as she acquainted herself with her new home. *Her new home.* Yes, whatever the future might hold in store for her, this was to be her new home.

'Do you like it?' Brenda's voice interrupted her thoughts, and there was a faint flush on Dale's cheeks as she swung round to face the woman.

'Oh, it's—it's beautiful,' she stammered helplessly, 'and I—I don't quite know how to thank you.'

'Don't try, my dear,' Brenda smiled warmly, then she turned towards her son and gestured to a space beside the door. 'Just leave everything there, Rick. I'll send Lucy up in a few minutes to unpack for Dale.'

'Oh, but—but that won't be necessary, I——'

'Don't worry about a thing, my dear,' she cut short Dale's protests. 'The bathroom is through there if you would like to freshen up.' She pointed in the direction of the white panelled door to her right. 'And I shall expect you downstairs in the living-room for tea in a few minutes.'

Dale nodded. 'Thank you.'

'Coming, Rick?' Brenda asked, glancing at the attorney.

'In a minute, Mother,' he replied tersely, and waited until Brenda had left the room before he turned to speak to Dale. 'While you're here I want you to think of this as your home. You can see the pool from your window. If you ever feel like having a swim, then please feel free to do so without having to ask someone's permission first. There's a tennis court as well, and if you want to ask a few of your friends over for a game, then you can do so at any time.'

Dale stared up into that immobile face for a moment, and swallowed at the sudden lump in her throat. 'You—you're being overwhelmingly kind.'

'Kindness is not one of my virtues, and you'll discover that before very long,' he said, and it sounded almost like a warning. 'I suggest you wash your hands and powder your nose, or whatever it is you want to do, and come downstairs for tea. The living-room is across the hall on your left as you come down.'

'Thank you.'

He turned on his heel and walked out of the room, closing the door quietly behind him, and relief quivered through her as she listened to his departing footsteps down the passage.

The bathroom was tiled in rose-pink and white to match the bedroom, and large mirrors reflected her image as she stepped inside. It was all so very beautiful that she felt as out of place as her battered suitcase on the expensive carpet in the bedroom. She studied her image briefly in the mirror, her glance sliding from her hair which she had tied back in a ponytail, down to the blue cotton frock which had lasted her through the previous summer, and she decided she looked like an ungainly rag doll in an antique china shop.

God had bestowed upon her a face and figure not worth glancing at twice. She ought to be grateful for the health and unexpected wealth which had come her way, but, as she washed her hands and splashed water on to her hot face, she could not help wishing for the unobtainable.

She dried her hands on the soft pink towel and dabbed lightly at her face, but she did not powder her nose as Rick Crawford had suggested. The nuns at St Stephen's had discouraged the use of make-up, and Dale had, quite frankly, never bothered much with her appearance. She was unattractive, and that was that, she had decided, and there had been no sense in attempting the impossible with make-up, or with anything else in the futile hope of looking more presentable.

In the living-room, over tea, it was Brenda Crawford who chattered gaily. Rick replied with little interest to many of the things she remarked upon, and Dale sat quietly on the edge of her upright antique chair, almost too afraid to breathe as she held the delicate china tea-cup in her hands.

'You must excuse me, but I have to get back to the office,' Rick said at length, rising to his feet and placing his cup in the tray before he glanced sharply at Dale. 'You and I will have a chat after dinner this evening. There are one or two matters we must discuss.'

Her tea-cup rattled in the saucer, and she curled her fingers about it hastily to silence the visible evidence of her nervousness. 'Yes, Mr . . . er . . . Rick.'

'It will come easier in time,' he mocked her stumbling effort to use his name. 'See you both later.'

'You mustn't be nervous of Rick, my dear,' Brenda said the moment they were alone. 'He appears to be a difficult man on the surface, but when you get to know him better you'll discover that he can be quite human.' She smiled with a hint of mischief in her eyes, then sobered once again. 'He carries such tremendous responsibilities, and it's inclined to make him boorish at times.'

Dale lowered her unhappy gaze to the cup she clutched so tightly in her hands, and she placed it carefully in the tray before she spoke. 'I'm afraid I've become an added responsibility to him.'

'Don't think of it that way, Dale,' the older woman said at once. 'I'm so happy to have you here with us that I can't begin to tell you what it will mean to me to have your company.'

Dale looked up into eyes observing her with warmth and sincerity. 'Thank you, Mrs Crawford.'

'I must go and see about dinner,' said Brenda, rising to her feet, 'but make yourself at home, Dale.'

'I think perhaps I'd like to go for a swim,' Dale replied, feeling considerably better than when she had arrived less than an hour ago.

'A good idea, child,' Brenda Crawford agreed as she picked up the tray and walked out of the living-room.

Dale followed her out at once and went up to her room. Her suitcase no longer stood on the carpeted floor, and the box, too, had disappeared, but her clothes had been packed away neatly in the wall cupboard with its white, slatted doors, and her much read, treasured collection of books had been stashed in an orderly fashion in the small bookshelf beside the writing desk.

She found her black one-piece swimsuit without much difficulty, and stripped hastily down to her skin. In time she hoped to acquire a less sombre-looking swimsuit, but for the moment she would have to make do with what she had, she decided as she wriggled herself into the plain, stretchy garment. She put her dress on over it and, taking her old towel with her, went downstairs in search of the pool Rick Crawford had mentioned.

The large, kidney-shaped swimming pool nestled amongst the trees below her bedroom window. It was tiled attractively with a mixture of blue and white tiles, and the water looked especially inviting on that hot and intensely humid afternoon. Dale stepped out of her sandals, and pulled her dress off over her head. She tugged at the narrow ribbon in her hair, and it fell free to hang down her back, then she walked towards the edge of the pool and plunged into the water in one fluid, graceful movement. Small and slender, she sliced through the water with an enviable ease and, as her heated body rejoiced in the coolness of the water, she forgot for a time about her formidable guardian, and the strangeness of having to adapt to a new life away from the protective walls of St Stephen's Academy.

She climbed out of the pool half an hour later, the water dripping off her arms and legs which had already acquired a golden tan, and moved with an unconscious grace as she walked to where she had left her towel draped over the back of a chair. She might not have been endowed with the conventional beauty of others, but there was an attractive air of mystery about her which would most certainly draw the attention of a keen, discerning eye. Her full, sensitive mouth suggested a tenderness and passion as yet unexplored, and the tilt of her head on her slender, swanlike neck hinted at a deep-seated pride. Her thin body, like a young sapling, was straight yet pliable, and the gentle curve of breasts and hips were undeniably feminine, but this was kept rigidly hidden beneath shapeless frocks as if it was something to be ashamed of.

She hastily put her dress on and pushed her feet into her sandals at the sound of a car coming up the drive. She could not be certain whether it was Rick Crawford, or a visitor for his mother, and she was still attempting to tie back her long, lanky hair when a step behind her on the concrete tiles made her swing round nervously.

'Hello?' smiled the fair, exquisitely-dressed woman who seemed to glide towards Dale with the practised ease of a model, but her grey eyes were cool and assessing. 'You must be Dale Palmer.'

'Yes,' Dale answered her, fumbling her hair into place, and aware of her cotton frock clinging to her damp swimsuit underneath.

'I'm Melissa Arnell,' the woman introduced herself, tilting her head at an angle so that the slanted rays of the late afternoon sun turned her fair hair to spun gold. 'When Rick told me about you I thought I'd come along and say "welcome".'

'Thank you,' Dale murmured politely, studying the woman facing her, and deciding that Melissa Arnell was so incredibly beautiful she might have been mistaken for a goddess.

'Hello, Melissa,' Brenda Crawford interrupted Dale's silent observation, and they both turned to see the older woman walking towards them with a vaguely reserved smile on her face. 'I wasn't expecting you.'

'Rick invited me over for dinner this evening,' Melissa explained, her perfume mingling with the scent of the roses ranking over the arbour close by. 'I hope you don't mind?'

'Not at all,' Brenda replied at once, then she glanced quickly at Dale. 'You'd better go up and change, my dear. Rick will be home soon, and we'll have dinner shortly afterwards.'

'Yes, Mrs Crawford,' Dale murmured obediently, faintly relieved to escape from the vision of beauty who seemed to be observing her so calculatingly.

She did not wait to listen in on more of their conversation, but sped towards the house before Rick arrived home, and he, too, found her looking like a drowned rat.

CHAPTER TWO

DALE washed her hair and changed for dinner into the only decent dress she possessed in her very sparse wardrobe. It was a beige frock, rather old-fashioned with puffy elbow-length sleeves, a white Peter Pan collar, and white buttons down the front of the bodice. A belt, of the same beige cotton as the frock, was fastened about her waist, and the image she presented in the mirror was agonisingly young for someone her age. She swept her hair back from her face and tied it in the nape of her neck with a narrow white ribbon, then she slipped her feet into white sandals with heels which added at least an inch to her height. Her face was devoid of make-up, but her youthful skin was creamy-smooth as it stretched firmly across high cheekbones down to her small, rounded chin, but it was not her face she was thinking of as she studied herself in the mirror. Sister Teresa had always liked her in this beige frock, and Dale had always felt that the style, although simple, did something for her, but her morale sank lower than the carpeted floor at her feet when she thought of the beautiful Melissa Arnell.

Brenda Crawford had said that she should go down to the living-room when she was ready and, taking a last despairing look at herself in the mirror, she left her room and went downstairs.

Rick and Melissa were in the living-room. Dale could hear the murmur of their voices as she crossed the hall, but, at the mention of her name, she paused with a measure of uncertainty, and realised that her soft-soled sandals on the carpeted floor had not warned them of her approach. They were discussing her, that much was obvious to Dale, and she hovered with indecision. Should she announce her presence in some way, or should she simply retrace her steps?

'She's really quite pathetically plain, poor thing,' Melissa's low, musical voice held Dale riveted to the floor. 'It really is too bad that you have to be saddled with her for the next two years, darling.'

Rick replied to that, but Dale was too swamped with humiliation and embarrassment at that moment to hear what he had said, and then Melissa was speaking once again.

'What *are* you going to do with her?'

'My dear Melissa, I'm not going to do anything with her which is not required of me. I shall see to it that she gets the education she requires, and I shall handle the legal side of her affairs until she's twenty-one,' Rick informed her tersely. 'After that it's entirely up to Dale what she does with herself *and* her inheritance.'

There was something so callous about the way he spoke that Dale felt the sting of hot tears behind her eyes, and she stood there, too afraid to move, and too afraid almost to breathe for fear of being discovered.

'Two years is an awfully long time for you to carry such a burden on your shoulders, Rick,' Melissa cruelly underlined the very thing that stabbed at Dale's pride.

'It will pass,' Rick answered abruptly, and Dale felt like an unwanted baggage which had been dumped on his doorstep. The feeling was not unfamiliar to her, but somehow it still had the power to hurt.

Not caring now whether they heard her or not, she retraced her steps and hurried upstairs, but Brenda Crawford emerged from her bedroom at the extreme end of the passage before Dale could reach the privacy of her own room.

'What's the matter, my dear?' she asked, studying

Dale's face with concern when she was a few paces away, but the light in the passage was fortunately too dim for her to notice the naked pain in those large blue eyes gazing back at her. 'I thought you'd be downstairs in the living-room.'

Sending up a swift prayer for forgiveness, Dale said untruthfully, 'I—I decided to wait for you, Mrs Crawford.'

'That was sweet of you, Dale,' she smiled, and her delicate perfume wafted about Dale as Brenda Crawford took her arm. 'Come along, my dear. Let's go down, shall we?'

Dale was silent throughout dinner, and kept her eyes fixedly on her plate even though she did little more than rearrange her food. She could not look at the beautiful Melissa Arnell; her beauty was a cruel reminder of Dale's 'pathetically plain' appearance, and least of all could she look at Rick Crawford, who had spoken so callously of his position as her guardian.

She excused herself from the table immediately after dinner, but when she got to her feet she found Rick barring her way.

'I want to see you in my study in an hour's time,' he said briskly. 'You'll find it across the hall.'

'Yes, Mr Crawford,' she replied obediently, forgetting for the moment to use his name, and she glanced up briefly to see the ominous tightening of his lips, but he said nothing as he stood aside for her to leave.

Dale went up to her room, but she did not switch on the light as she closed the door behind her and walked across to the window. She liked the darkness; it was kind and soft as a blanket, and she leaned out of the window to stare down at the almost fluorescent pool below. It was a warm, sultry night, and in the moonlight the water looked inviting, but she would have to delay the pleasure of a swim on that star-studded night. Rick Crawford had instructed her to be in his study within an hour, and she still had enough pride and dignity left within her not to want to confront him with her hair still dripping wet after a swim.

The murmur of voices below made her draw back sharply from the window. It was Rick and Melissa; Dale would know that soft, liltingly feminine laughter anywhere and, very carefully, she adjusted her position so that she could observe them without being seen. Melissa's arm was linked through Rick's as they walked slowly towards the pool. They were talking softly, their heads close together as if their conversation was of a personal and intimate nature, and Dale was almost too afraid to breathe when they stopped directly below her window. Melissa laughed softly once again at something Rick had said, then she turned into his arms, her body curving seductively into his, and Dale stood transfixed as Rick lowered his head and kissed Melissa. Dale watched them with a peculiar tightness in her chest. She wanted desperately to move away from the window, but her legs refused to move for some reason, and she stood there in the darkness like a frozen statue until they finally moved away and entered the house through the patio doors.

Dale sagged weakly against the wall, guilt swamping her at having observed those moments of intimacy between them, then she crossed the room jerkily to switch on the light. She tried to read until it was time for her to go downstairs for her confrontation with Rick in his study, but she could not concentrate on a single word, and simply sat there with the book in her lap while the small clock on the bedside table ticked away the minutes.

The door to Rick's study stood open, making it easier for Dale to find it, and she hovered nervously in the doorway until he looked up from the papers before him and saw her standing there.

'Come in, Dale, and close the door behind you,' he ordered, and she obeyed in silence, wishing she could rid herself of the mental picture of that embrace she had witnessed from her bedroom window. He gestured her into a leather armchair, and she sat down gingerly, perching nervously on the edge of it as his eyes flicked over her pale, sober features. 'You must be tired, so I won't keep you long, but I want you to know that you'll receive a monthly allowance until you're able to support yourself. If you should require anything over and above that allowance, then I must insist that you discuss the matter with me, and please don't hesitate to do so, as the money is there for your use. It's simply that the legal aspect of a situation such as this is always involved, and large sums of money are not always readily available unless your request has my stamp of approval on it.'

'I understand,' she said politely, avoiding his eyes and glancing instead at the rows of legal books displayed so impressively in the shelves behind him.

'Do you drive a car?' he shot the question at her, and his compelling eyes drew hers relentlessly back to his.

'Sister Teresa taught me, and I got my driver's licence when I turned eighteen.'

'In that case we shall have to see about buying you a small car for your own use.' The look of surprise on her face made him add bluntly, 'You're going to need one next year when you go to the secretarial college.'

'Yes, I—I suppose so. Thank you,' she stammered nervously.

'Do you have any particular make of car in mind?'

'It—It doesn't really matter,' she shook her head. 'Anything will do.'

'You'll leave the choice to me, then?'

'Yes, of course.'

'Good,' he said abruptly, taking a bulky envelope

out of his desk drawer and placing it on the desk in front of her. 'That's this month's allowance. I suggest you open a savings account somewhere, and please remember what I said about coming to me if there's anything else you may require.'

'I'll remember,' she promised.

'I think that was all I had to discuss with you,' he dismissed her. 'You may go.'

'Goodnight,' she murmured, getting to her feet with a nervous haste that propelled her towards the door.

'Dale?' She stopped and turned to find him standing directly behind her with an envelope in the hand he extended towards her. 'You forgot this.'

'Oh—Oh, yes, I—I'm sorry,' she stammered, flustered and embarrassed, and horrified to see that her hand was shaking as she took the envelope from him.

'Goodnight, Dale.'

She looked up, saw the laughter in his eyes, and fled as her heightened embarrassment sent the redness surging up into her cheeks.

She did not sleep very well that night. She could not decide whether it was the strangeness of her surroundings, or the anxiety with which she viewed the future, but she was awake very early the following morning when she heard someone diving into the pool, and thrashing about in the water. She leapt out of bed in her flannel nightgown, and hurried across to the window, but fell back a pace when she realised that it was Rick.

He sliced through the water, his strong arms propelling him at speed from one end of the pool to the other, and he swam several vigorous lengths before he climbed out and walked to where he had left his towel. His body was deeply tanned, and not an ounce of superfluous flesh marred his magnificent physique. He looked deceptively lean in a suit, but in blue swimming trunks his well-muscled body suggested a ripcord strength, and she watched him unashamedly while he dried himself. The muscles rippled across his back and along his arms with every movement, and the oddest sensations began to stir within her. He disappeared into the house some minutes later, and it was only as she expelled the air slowly from her lungs that she realised she had been holding her breath in some sort of awed wonder. For the second time in less than twelve hours she had observed Rick Crawford from her window without him knowing, but on this occasion she felt elated about it instead of guilty.

Rick had already had his breakfast by the time Dale went downstairs, and from Mrs Crawford she gathered that he was in his study going over a brief before he left for the office.

'Eat your breakfast, my dear, then we're going shopping,' Brenda instructed when Dale lingered over her egg and bacon.

'Shopping?'

'You need a complete new wardrobe, Dale,' the older woman smiled into Dale's surprised eyes. 'The festive season is virtually on our doorstep, and you're going to need clothes for next year as well.'

'I did think of buying one or two dresses,' Dale admitted thoughtfully, popping a piece of toast in her mouth.

'Then hurry up, my dear, and let's get to town before there's not a parking space to be had.'

Dale felt vaguely disappointed at not seeing Rick before they left the house, but the excitement of buying new clothes soon dominated all other feelings that morning as she drove into town with Brenda Crawford in her small Mazda.

She soon discovered that Mrs Crawford had no intention of calling a halt to their shopping spree after the two dresses had been purchased. At least a dozen more were selected, for day and evening wear, and this was followed up by several sets of underwear of the finest silk.

'Mrs Crawford, I couldn't possibly buy all these things!' Dale protested when Brenda instructed the shop assistant to parcel up every single item they had selected. 'I haven't enough money to pay for them.'

'The account will be sent to Rick.'

'Oh, but we can't do that!' Dale gasped nervously. 'He told me last night that if I wanted to spend money like this I would have to consult him first.'

Brenda Crawford smiled tolerantly. 'Rick is well aware of what we're doing this morning, my dear, and it was *he* who suggested that the account be sent directly to him.'

'You—You mean he gave permission for me to buy all—all these clothes?' Dale stammered, bewildered and delighted at the same time.

'That's right,' Brenda nodded, taking Dale's arm and ushering her towards the shoe department of the fashionable boutique. 'Isn't it exciting?'

Mischief danced in her eyes, and Dale found herself returning that smile with a lightheartedness she had not felt in weeks.

Their shopping expedition had taken up so much of their time that they had lunch in town, and when they finally went home, the back seat of the Mazda was loaded with parcels of all shapes and sizes. Dale had never possessed so many clothes in her life before, and such extravagance was totally unheard of. Sister Teresa would have clutched her rosary and rolled her eyes towards the heavens had she been there, but then, of course, Dale's parents had left her sufficient money only for the bare necessities, and Dale had never needed or wanted more.

Lucy came out to help them carry the parcels into the house, and her black face was smiling almost from ear to ear. 'I will put everything away for you, young missus.'

'Thank you, Lucy,' Dale smiled back at her, then she followed Brenda into the living-room where a jug of iced fruit juice awaited them.

'Oh, dear!' Brenda muttered when they had quenched their thirst, and when Dale glanced at her questioningly she gestured towards the filmy object which was draped across the back of the sofa. 'Melissa left her wrap here last night.'

'Miss Arnell is very beautiful,' Dale spoke her thoughts aloud.

'Do you really think so?'

'Yes,' Dale replied without hesitation, glancing at the older woman curiously. 'Don't you?'

'I suppose one could say she is beautiful, yes, but it's a cold, hard beauty that doesn't appeal very much to me.' A look of vague dissatisfaction flashed across Brenda's controlled features. 'Real beauty comes from within.'

'Sister Teresa always said that,' Dale acknowledged absently.

'And she was right too,' Brenda smiled across at her. 'Believe me.'

'What does Miss Arnell do?' Dale probed curiously.

'She's a photographic model.'

'I should have guessed as much,' Dale nodded, and once again she was plagued by that mental picture of Melissa Arnell in Rick's arms. 'Is she going to marry Rick?'

'*I hope not!*' Brenda remarked with such emphasis that Dale jumped nervously. 'One never can tell, of course. Rick's a strange man, and very much like his father used to be. He has an eye for beauty these days, and I don't deny that, but he's not always sensible where beautiful women are concerned.'

Dale was beginning to suspect that Brenda did not

like the beautiful Melissa Arnell very much. She had spoken of her beauty as being cold and hard, and Dale found that a little confusing.

'Has he known Miss Arnell a long time?' she continued to question the woman seated opposite her, and she could not even explain to herself why this should interest her so much.

'Rick has known her since her divorce a few months ago.'

'She was married?'

'Yes,' Brenda nodded, 'and to a very nice man, I believe, but the marriage just didn't work out . . . or so I'm told.'

Dale considered this for a moment in thoughtful silence, then she decided to step off the subject which was beginning to distress her immensely. 'I think I'll go for a swim and try out my new swimsuit.'

'Don't stay out in the sun too long,' Brenda warned, and a new warmth invaded Dale's heart at this display of concern.

For the first time someone other than Sister Teresa had shown that they cared, and Dale hugged that feeling to her almost jealously.

The next few weeks passed with comparative ease, and Dale settled down to a comfortable relationship with Rick Crawford and his mother. She was no longer so very nervous in Rick's company, and neither did his terse, often abrupt manner disturb her to the extent it had in the beginning.

Rick's sister, Alexis Murray, arrived three days before Christmas. She was a widow, and five years older than Rick, so Brenda Crawford had told Dale some time ago, and Dale found herself liking this tall, slender woman with the laughing eyes, and hair which was as dark as Rick's except for a sprinkling of grey at the temples.

'I'm glad I've met you at last,' Alexis told Dale when they sat out on the terrace before dinner that first evening after her arrival. 'I've heard so much about you from Mother.'

'I've heard so much about you, too,' Dale confessed. 'I believe you've written several books on South Africa, and that you are now busy collecting information for a book on trees and shrubs of Natal.'

'That's correct,' Alexis smiled, her dark eyes appraising Dale intently. 'Are you interested in plants?'

'I've never given it much thought,' Dale replied truthfully.

'Be careful, Dale,' Rick warned, handing them each a glass of wine. 'When Alex starts talking about her work, she never knows when to stop!'

Despite the mockery in his voice, the shortening of his sister's name suggested a deep affection, and Dale could not help but envy them.

'Is that so?' Alex demanded haughtily. 'And what about when you get on to your legal hobbyhorse?'

'The law is a very interesting subject.'

'I can say the same about *my* work,' Alex argued.

A faint smile curved Rick's thin mouth. 'We'll never agree on this subject.'

'Do we ever agree on *any* subject?' Alex quipped back mockingly.

'We both like Tchaikovsky,' Rick proffered.

'Indeed we do,' his sister smiled humorously.

'Do you always argue like this?' Dale asked after sitting there quietly listening to the friendly bantering between them.

'Always,' Alex stated firmly. 'But we never argue about important things.'

'Important things?' Dale queried a little confusedly.

'When I need legal advice I would never dream of going to anyone else but Rick,' Alex replied, slanting a wry smile in her brother's direction. 'He's a very clever attorney, even if I have to say so myself.'

Rick, who had been leaning nonchalantly against one of the stone pillars, bowed gallantly in his sister's direction just as Brenda Crawford joined them for a glass of wine before dinner, and the conversation drifted in a different direction after that.

Dale was unaccustomed to the gaiety which prevailed around the dinner table that evening, and Rick, usually so stern, relaxed to the extent that he actually smiled on several occasions. It made him look much younger than his thirty-five years, and she found herself wishing that he would smile more often.

No one got to bed before eleven that evening, but Dale, by nature an early riser, was awake again at five-thirty the following morning, and leaning with her elbows on the windowsill when Rick stepped out on to the sunlit patio beneath her. He loosened the towel about his lean hips, and looked up suddenly as if he had sensed her presence.

Too startled to move, she continued to stare down into those faintly mocking eyes until he said: 'Why don't you come down and have a swim before anyone else invades the pool?'

Dale was tempted, but she hesitated for some reason to accept his invitation. 'Well, I . . .'

'Come on,' he interrupted her impatiently. 'Don't waste time, and get down here fast!'

That last bit sounded very much like an order, and Dale obeyed instinctively. She slipped out of her silky nightdress, and pulled on her new blue and white swimsuit. Her towel she tied sarong-style about her, then she went downstairs as quietly and quickly as she could.

Rick was floating lazily in the centre of the pool when she stepped out on to the patio and, impatient for the coolness of the water on that already humid morning, she draped her towel over a chair and plunged into the pool to swim underwater almost the length of the pool before she surfaced.

'I'm glad to see you're not one of those girls who stand on the edge of the pool for ages before attempting to get into the water,' Rick remarked as he swam alongside her until their hands touched the marble edge.

'I love swimming,' she confessed, pushing her hair out of her eyes.

'And you do it very well,' he complimented her. 'I'll race you to the other side.'

The challenge was unexpected, but her reflexes were in first class shape, and they kicked themselves away from the side almost simultaneously. Dale was a strong swimmer, but Rick was far stronger, and he reached the opposite side seconds before her. She felt exhilaratingly alive for some reason, and she was breathless and laughing when he ducked her head under the water as a penalty for losing.

'Are you happy here, Dale?' he asked eventually when they had exhausted themselves and were sitting on the edge of the pool with their legs dangling in the water.

'Everyone has been very kind to me,' she replied carefully, averting her eyes from his broad chest where the short dark hair curled against his damp brown skin.

'That doesn't exactly answer my question.'

'And your legal mind wants everything tied up into neat little packages labelled "affirmative" and "negative".'

'That's correct,' he said abruptly. 'That way there can be no misunderstandings.'

She looked away from him, out across the pool and beyond, while she tried to decide how to answer him, but she knew that only the truth would suffice with Rick.

'I'm happy here,' she said at last, unaware of that note of melancholy in her soft voice. 'It's the nearest thing to a real home I've ever known. I only wish that . . .'

'Go on,' he urged, studying her intently with those dark, disturbing eyes. 'Don't stop now that I've at last got you to talk.'

'I only wish I didn't have to be such a burden to you,' she complied, recalling that hateful conversation she had overheard between him and Melissa Arnell.

'I've told you once before——'

'Yes, I know,' she interrupted him, gesturing helplessly with her hands. 'You said that you wouldn't have brought me here if you'd considered I would be an inconvenience, but I can't help feeling like an intruder in your home sometimes.'

His strong fingers gripped her chin, and turned her face up to his so that she had no option but to look into those unfathomable eyes. 'I ought to be very angry with you, do you know that?'

'You wanted the truth, the whole truth, and nothing but the truth,' she smiled shakily.

'I don't think of you as an intruder,' he said, his eyes holding hers captive, and his fingers moving in a light caress against her jaw. 'Over the past three weeks I have, in fact, begun to think of you as part of the family, and I would like you to feel that way about us too.'

He meant it; she could see it in his eyes and hear it in his voice, but her wary heart needed assurance. 'You—you really mean that?'

He smiled as he released her chin and raised his right hand in the air as one would do in court to take a solemn oath. 'It's the truth, the whole truth, and nothing but the truth, so help me God.'

A warmth invaded her heart that made it swell with happiness and, with a new-found confidence, she flung a laughing challenge at him as she plunged into the water. 'Race you back to the other side!'

Caught off guard, Rick was several seconds late off the mark, but it gave Dale the advantage she needed, and this time she reached the other side before him.

'You cheated!' he accused, looking boyish with his hair plastered against his broad forehead as he surfaced beside her.

'I know,' she laughed impishly as she splashed water rather daringly into his face.

A devilish gleam entered his eyes, and there was no knowing what he might have done if Alex had not arrived on the scene at that precise moment.

'Is there any room in that pool for me?' she asked teasingly.

'Plenty, if you're quick about it,' Rick replied, his attention diverted from Dale long enough for her to put a safe distance between them.

Alex slipped out of her towelling robe and for a woman of forty Dale noticed that she still had a remarkably good figure in a swimsuit. She was attractive and intelligent, and Dale could not help wondering why she had never married again after her husband had died.

They cooled off in the pool for at least half an hour before they went inside and changed for breakfast. Rick had to go out for a while, and Dale suspected that he went to see Melissa, but he surprisingly did not stay away too long, and returned shortly after tea that morning.

'Come with me,' he instructed Dale when he found her in the kitchen seasoning the turkey while Alex and Brenda prepared the sauce for the Christmas pudding. 'I have something to show you.'

Dale rinsed her hands under the tap in the basin and wiped them dry before she took off her apron, then she followed him out of the house with a puzzled look on her face.

As they rounded the corner nearest to the garages Dale realised how wrong she had been to think that he had been with Melissa. Under the pergola stood a pale blue Volkswagen Golf, and her breath caught in her throat as she stared at it. She paused abruptly in her stride, but Rick dangled the keys in front of her eyes almost as one would tempt a donkey with a carrot.

'It's yours,' he announced abruptly. 'Signed, sealed, delivered—and bought with your own money, in case you were wondering.'

She took the keys from him and walked slowly towards the car, and there was a sparkle of excitement in her eyes as she ran her fingers lightly over the gleaming bonnet.

'I've never owned anything before.'

'You do now,' Rick said directly behind her. 'You own considerably more than simply this car.'

She was momentarily speechless, and the sparkle left her eyes as she turned slowly to face him. 'You sound bitter, and perhaps a little angry. Am I the cause of it?'

'No, you're not.' He brushed his knuckles lightly against her cheek. 'I don't think you've had a fair deal in life, and it makes me a little angry to think of it.'

She was deeply touched by what he had said, but she was also a little on the defensive. 'I haven't been totally unhappy, Rick.'

'But you haven't been totally happy either,' he countered tersely, his dark gaze holding hers for what seemed like an eternity, then he lowered his head abruptly and kissed her with unexpected tenderness on her soft, parted lips. The contact was brief, but she was still struggling with an odd shortness of breath when Rick calmly walked round to the passenger side of the car. 'Let's take it for a run to see how it handles on the road.'

Dale's hands were shaking visibly when she inserted

the key into the ignition and turned it, but she had complete control of herself when the engine purred to life. Sister Teresa had been an excellent teacher, and Rick could not fault Dale as she reversed the Golf into the driveway before putting it into a forward gear and driving it out through the gates.

The small car handled smoothly, and although Dale was intensely aware of Rick's tall frame seated so close beside her, she felt not a scrap of nervousness as she drove into the city and back again to Westville as Rick had instructed.

'How does it feel?' he asked when she parked it under the shady pergola once more.

'Wonderful!' she told him with an unsteady laugh, then she slanted a mischievous glance at him. 'Are you satisfied now that I shan't go out there and injure myself?'

'You're a clever little witch,' he laughed dryly, turning in his seat to observe her through narrowed eyes. 'You knew all the time that I wanted to make sure your driving was up to scratch, didn't you?'

'I never gave it a thought at first,' she admitted, undoing her seat belt and letting it slide into place. 'I began to suspect it, though, when you insisted that I should drive through Durban on a day when almost everybody was out doing their last-minute Christmas shopping.'

'Well, you passed with flying colours, young Dale, and I compliment you on your expertise.' He smiled twistedly. 'Or should I compliment your Sister Teresa on her expertise as a teacher?'

'I think Sister Teresa deserves all the credit,' she replied gravely. 'I was a very bad pupil in the beginning, but her wonderful patience was finally rewarded.'

Rick did not reply to that, but as they walked back to the house, he said: 'You've gained a little bit of independence today, but don't treat it lightly, will you?'

Was there a warning lurking there somewhere, or did she imagine it? She glanced up at him swiftly, but his face had assumed that immobile mask she was beginning to know so well, and uncertainty settled upon her once more like a heavy blanket. Her confidence in herself slithered down to zero, and she withdrew into her shell with a familiarity which was almost comforting. Nothing could touch her when she was in that private world of her own, but although she felt safe, she also felt incredibly lonely walking beside this man who could be her friend one minute, and a stranger the next. If she tried hard enough she could almost feel again the warmth of his hard mouth against her own during that brief kiss, but she did not particularly want to think about it. It had meant nothing to him; it had been the sort of kiss he would have bestowed on a child, but it had awakened something within her which she knew she would never be entirely free of in future.

CHAPTER THREE

CHRISTMAS that year had been the most enjoyable Dale had ever experienced, but she could not let it pass without a visit to St Stephen's. There had, after all, been so much to tell Sister Teresa. The exam results had been published shortly before New Year's Day, and there had been cause once again to celebrate when it was discovered that Dale had passed with three distinctions to her name.

'You ought to go to university,' Rick had said when he studied her results, but Dale had remained adamant. She had no interest in an academic career of any nature.

She settled in quite happily with the Crawfords, and her first two terms at the secretarial college had slipped by with incredible speed. Much against Rick's wishes, Dale had found herself a 'mornings only' job during the July holidays, and that left her free in the afternoons to laze about in the sun, or to sketch the surrounding countryside to her heart's content.

She was beginning to think of Rick's home as her own, and going to college was almost therapeutic. She was discovering that she was not so very different from any of the other girls, except in her appearance perhaps, but they had accepted her as she was, and although she had not acquired a special friend, she had a small circle of acquaintances whom she occasionally invited home for a game of tennis. If Rick had to ask her now whether she was happy, then she could quite honestly have said that she was happier than she had ever been before, but she seldom saw Rick, except at dinner in the evenings and weekends, and then

Melissa Arnell was always there, making it impossible for Dale to approach him.

Brenda Crawford made up admirably for her son's neglect, and they quite often drove out to Amanzimtoti to spend the weekend with Alex in her home on the hill which overlooked the beach. Those weekends were memorable occasions for Dale, and she often envied Alex her view of the sea. Her spacious garden was a paradise on earth where flamboyant and African tulip trees flowered almost on her doorstep, and Dale seldom came away from there without having made a few sketches of her picturesque surroundings.

There had been no warning prior to the incident which robbed Dale of her still fragile confidence in herself, and Brenda Crawford would have been inconsolably distressed had she known that she had been the instrument which had triggered off the unfortunate and shocking discovery.

It happened during the final week of the July holidays. Brenda was writing letters on the shady terrace, and Dale chose to join her there with one of her favourite books to spend a lazy afternoon reading. 'Are you doing anything special this afternoon?' Brenda asked eventually, her smiling glance sliding over the young girl's youthful figure which had filled out so attractively over the past months.

'Nothing worth mentioning,' Dale smiled back at her, gesturing vaguely with the book in her hand. 'Was there something you wanted me to do?'

'I'm writing a few letters, and I was hoping you could go off and post them for me.'

'I'll do that with pleasure.'

'The only problem is,' Brenda announced ruefully, 'I haven't any envelopes.'

'Shall I go out and buy some for you?' Dale offered at once.

'No, I don't think so,' the older woman shook her

head. 'I've put it down on my shopping list, but for the moment I think you might find envelopes in Rick's study. He usually keeps a supply in his desk drawers, and I'm certain he won't miss three.' She smiled almost conspiratorially at Dale. 'Would you mind getting them for me while I finish off this letter?'

'I'll be back in a moment,' Dale promised, leaving her book on the cane table and going into the house.

It was not often that she found cause to enter Rick's study unless it was at his request, or to search for something to read, but she had never ventured near his desk before without his knowledge. The envelopes were in one of the drawers, Brenda had said, and Dale opened the first drawer to encounter several legal-looking files which had been neatly tied with red tape. She closed that drawer swiftly and opened another, but it contained a tape recorder which she presumed he used for dictation. It was only in the fourth drawer that she found the envelopes she required, but something which had been thrust into the back of the drawer caught her eye. It was an envelope addressed to Rick in her father's handwriting, and her curiosity was so intense that she reached into the drawer and took it out. She stared at the envelope undecidedly for several seconds while she laboured under a feeling of guilt, but, tempted beyond reason, she extracted the letter and opened it carefully.

The letter was dated two years ago, and the address was a chalet somewhere in Switzerland, but Dale skimmed over it uninterestedly in favour of reading the contents. She read through it quickly, afraid of being caught prying into someone else's personal correspondence, but when she came to the end of the letter she was pale and shaken, with a stricken look in her eyes. She sat down heavily in Rick's swivel armchair, and read the letter through once again as if to make sure that she had not misunderstood, but it had been unnecessary, for every word had been imprinted on her tortured mind as if with a white hot branding iron.

Dear Rick, her father had written. *I would like to express my deepest sympathy to you and your family on the death of your father. He was not only my attorney, but also my friend and adviser.*

As you may know, I had nominated your father as my daughter's guardian and, as an attorney yourself, you must realise that this is a matter which must now be rectified. I can think of no one else but yourself whom I can trust to nominate as Dale's guardian and, if you are agreeable to this, I hope you will make the necessary alterations.

Dale is not our child, of course. My wife could never have children, and she refused to adopt one, but when Emily, my poor demented young sister, died in the sanatorium shortly after giving birth to her illegitimate child, we had no option but to adopt Dale, and my wife resented her from the start.

My work takes me all over the world, and my wife, Celeste, has always insisted on accompanying me. We tried to make a home for Dale at first, but Celeste could not tolerate the child, and I personally found her an embarrassment because of the circumstances of her birth. In the end Celeste suggested that we place the child at St Stephen's Academy, and the nuns have taken wonderful care of her all these years. Dale is a clever, intelligent girl, but she is withdrawn and lacks ambition in my opinion.

Because of the nature of my work, and the risk involved in travelling, I feel it is necessary that I should appoint someone as Dale's guardian and legal adviser. If something should happen to my wife and myself, then Dale will need someone to take care of her who could administrate her inheritance until she comes of age.

I trust you will accept this responsibility as your father did before you, and look forward to hearing from you. Yours faithfully, Ivan Palmer.

Dale's hands were shaking when she returned the letter, intact, to the drawer. She felt shocked and sick to the very core of her being as her fragile security crumbled beneath her. She had always known that she had been unwanted, but she had never dreamed . . . ! She shuddered, and a wave of revulsion swept through her to leave her feeling nauseated.

Picking up the envelopes Brenda had wanted, she walked, out of the study and closed the door behind her, but her feet felt like pieces of lead attached to the ends of her legs, and her shoulders sagged beneath the burden of this horrifying discovery.

'You're as white as a sheet,' Brenda remarked concernedly when Dale handed her the envelopes. 'Are you ill, my dear?'

'I have a headache,' Dale lied desperately. 'I'll take a few tablets and lie down for a while before I post your letters, if you don't mind.'

'Perhaps I should call the doctor.'

'That won't be necessary,' Dale protested hastily. 'I'll be all right in a little while.'

Alone in her room, she tried desperately to assimilate the facts, and to come to terms with them, but it was not an easy task adapting to the knowledge that the people she had always thought of as her parents, were *not* her parents at all. Ivan Palmer had been her *uncle*; the man who had given her a name because she had been born the illegitimate child of his young sister. Dale had always known how Celeste had felt about her, but she had always thought that Ivan had cared for her in some way. Now she knew the truth. She had been an embarrassment to him because of the circumstances of her birth, and he had been only too willing to rid himself of it at his wife's insistence. Celeste had been beautiful, a woman any man would have been proud to show off to his friends and colleagues, but Dale had been born plain and unattractive. Added to this she had been his sister's illegitimate child, and this had been too much for a man as proud as Ivan Palmer. He had done his duty, he had adopted her, but she had been nothing but an embarrassment and . . . !

'God, help me!' Dale prayed aloud as she fell to her knees beside her bed. 'I'm so confused!'

The shock of discovering the truth about herself had overshadowed one other important factor which was to affect her future, but now the words suddenly came tumbling into her mind. *Demented—sanatorium! Mad,* Dale's tormented mind added of its own volition. *Mad!* Emily Palmer had died in a sanatorium after giving birth to her illegitimate child, and she had died a demented woman. Was this insanity hereditary? She would have to find out! But even if it was *not*, there would always be that stigma attached to her name.

Dale passed a shaky hand over her white face as another revelation hit her with a stunning force. *Rick knew everything!* He knew that she had been adopted by her uncle, he knew that she was illegitimate, and he knew . . . oh, he *knew* about her mother's mental instability!

Nausea surged up from her stomach, but she fought it down. What must Rick think of her—what *did* he think of her? Was he the only one who knew about her, or was the rest of the family also aware of this cloud of shame under which she had been born?

Dale suddenly developed a pounding headache to give truth to the lie she had told Brenda Crawford, and she swallowed down a couple of aspirins in the hope that it would ease off. She had survived many setbacks in her life, and she would survive this as well, but nothing had ever hit her as hard as this before. She had inherited a past that was blacker than the blackest night, and heaven only knew how she was going to face the future.

She was still pale, but she was composed when she eventually went downstairs to collect Brenda's letters. 'I might be a while,' she warned. 'I haven't seen Sister Teresa since Christmas, and I might just pay her a visit.'

'Do that, my dear,' Brenda agreed, 'but please be home before dark. You know how Rick feels about you driving around alone after sunset.'

'I shan't be late,' Dale promised.

She *had* to talk to Sister Teresa, she was the only one who would understand, and it was with this thought in mind that Dale drove to St Stephen's that afternoon, stopping only to post the letters on the way.

Sister Teresa was in consultation with Mother Superior when Dale arrived at the Academy, but her face lit up with a smile when she finally emerged from the priory office to find Dale waiting for her.

'My child, how lovely it is to see you again!' she exclaimed softly, her hands outstretched in welcome.

'I must talk to you privately,' Dale whispered, gripping those pale fingers tightly, and Sister Teresa ushered her without hesitation or query into the small lounge used for visitors.

'We won't be disturbed here,' she said, closing the door and turning to face Dale. 'What is it, child?'

Dale wrung her hands in distress. 'I don't quite know where to start, or how to tell you.'

'Start at the beginning, child, and simply tell it as it comes,' Sister Teresa said quietly, seating herself on an upright chair and folding her hands in her lap in characteristic fashion.

Her calmness seemed to inject itself into Dale, and while she related her discovery, haltingly at first,

Sister Teresa's brown eyes observed her intently. The words finally flowed from Dale like water from a tap, and she poured out her misery until there was nothing left except the new fears and doubts which would not be stilled.

Dale stood rigid and tense during the brief silence that followed her lengthy account of what had occurred earlier that afternoon, then something snapped within her, and she fell to her knees beside Sister Teresa, burying her tortured face in that long white habit.

'Oh, Sister Teresa, I'm so unhappy!' Dale sobbed brokenly.

'You poor child.'

Sister Teresa did not attempt to coax Dale out of her tearful state. Experience had taught her that tears were sometimes necessary to cleanse the soul, and she sat there calmly, her hand resting gently on Dale's head until her sobs no longer echoed round the small room.

'What am I going to do?' Dale whispered at length when she had managed to control herself to some extent.

'Does knowing the truth make such a terrible difference?'

'It might.' Dale raised anxious, red-rimmed eyes to Sister Teresa's. 'Is insanity hereditary?'

'In some instances, yes.' Sister Teresa's glance softened at the stricken look on Dale's face. 'My child, do you think that, if there had been anything the matter with you mentally, I wouldn't have noticed it over the years?'

'But what if . . . one day when I'm married . . . what if my children . . . ?'

'Dale!' Sister Teresa shook her veiled head reprovingly. 'You don't know if your mother's ailment was hereditary.'

'But what if it was?' Dale spoke her worst fear aloud.

'You can't build your future on supposition,' the nun warned wisely. 'I suggest you discuss this with Mr Crawford.'

'No . . . *oh, no!*' Dale leapt to her feet, her eyes wide and desperate in her pale face. 'He's the last person I could *ever* talk to!'

'I don't understand.'

Dale stared at her. How could she speak of what lay in her heart when she had no way of explaining it even to herself? She had come to know Rick over the past six months. She knew what made him smile, and she knew what would make him angry. But would she be able to bear his anger once he discovered that she had stumbled across the truth? Would she be able to tolerate the pity he had kept so well hidden?

'I don't understand it myself,' she finally confessed in a whisper. 'I only know that I can't discuss this with him.'

'Dale, my child, I wish it was within my power to help you.'

Sister Teresa had risen to her feet, and Dale kissed her impulsively on the cheek, then she glanced at the time on the wrist watch Rick had given her for Christmas.

'I have to go,' she said. 'May I use the chapel before I leave?'

Sister Teresa smiled and nodded. 'The chapel doors will always be open to you, child.'

Dale knelt in prayer in the quiet chapel with its stained glass windows, and a new calmness had settled within her when she walked away from it fifteen minutes later.

Melissa Arnell came to dinner that evening, and she looked breathtakingly beautiful in an emerald green silk evening gown trimmed with the finest, most intricate lace. From their conversation Dale gathered that Rick was taking her to the theatre after dinner, and envy, inexplicable and fierce, stabbed at her as she made a pretence of eating.

'You're looking rather bleak this evening, Dale. Did your boy-friend walk out on you?' Melissa wanted to know when their coffee had been served, and she followed up her remark with soft laughter that rang mockingly in Dale's ears.

She tried to shrug off Melissa's observation, but she was too perilously close to tears and, pushing back her chair, she got jerkily to her feet. 'If you'll excuse me, Mrs Crawford, I'd like to go up to my room.'

'Yes, of course, Dale,' Brenda murmured concernedly.

Dale felt Rick's eyes burning into her back as she walked out of the dining-room, but she squared her shoulders and managed somehow to look outwardly calm and composed. It was only when she reached the stairs that she quickened her pace, and she burst into her room in a breathless rush seconds later.

There was no need to switch on the light. The moon was full, and it bathed the room in a silvery glow which was strangely soothing. This was not the first time Melissa had made such subtle yet pointed remarks about Dale's appearance. In the past Dale had been able to shrug it off and forget it, but on this particular evening she was totally vulnerable. Melissa knew very well that Dale did not possess such a thing as a boy-friend. 'Who would look at me anyway?' Dale muttered to herself. 'Who would look at me, the illegitimate daughter of a demented woman, when there are so many beautiful girls around?'

A lump rose in her throat, but she swallowed it down hastily. Self-pity was unhealthy, Sister Teresa had always said, and now Dale knew why. It made one feel a hundred times worse than one ought to.

She walked across the room towards the window, but a tap on her door made her swing round nervously and hastily switch on the bedside light.

'Come in,' she called apprehensively, and her heart leapt uncomfortably when Rick walked into her room and closed the door firmly behind him.

This was the first time he had entered her bedroom since the day she arrived, and in his dark evening suit he looked so dynamic and so vitally male that her knees went a little weak at the sight of him.

'What's wrong, Dale?' he asked, crossing the room towards her. 'Did something happen today that's upset you?'

He was standing so close to her that his masculine cologne seemed to be all around her, and it stirred her senses in a way it had never done before. She had the most extraordinary desire to fling herself into his arms, but she controlled it with an effort and turned from him to stare out of the window without actually seeing the pool or the moonlit garden below.

'Please don't be concerned about me. I'm really quite well,' she told him in her usually calm voice.

'Your happiness *is* my concern, and if something happened to upset you, then I hope you'll tell me about it,' Rick contradicted her. 'Mother tells me you complained of a headache this afternoon.'

'I took something for it, and it went away.'

'You hardly touched your food this evening.'

'I—I wasn't very hungry.'

'Look at me when you speak to me, and tell me the truth,' he instructed, his deep voice suddenly harsh, and his hands hurting her shoulders as he turned her roughly to face him.

'I'm not in the witness-box, and I don't tell lies,' she stated quietly, raising her eyes no higher than the tiny pearl buttons on his ruffled shirt front.

'You may not tell lies, little Dale, but you're being suspiciously evasive.'

'Please stop cross-examining me, Rick,' she begged desperately.

'Just answer one more question,' he insisted, his fingers beneath her chin forcing her to meet the onslaught of his dark, probing eyes. 'Are you feeling ill in any way?'

'I'm not ill.'

He stared down at her comtemplatively for a moment, then he nodded abruptly. 'I would like you to trust me, Dale. I have only your best interests at heart, and if you're ever troubled about anything, then I would like to think you trust me enough to discuss your problems with me.'

She stood perfectly still while his fingers caressed her cheek almost absently, but something stirred within her; something warm, tender and vibrant. She knew instinctively that it had to be curbed, and she fought against it valiantly, but, like a ship breaking free of its moorings in a storm, it surged like a tidal wave through her to leave her trembling inwardly with the force of it.

She drew a careful, steadying breath. 'Don't keep Melissa waiting, you know how she hates it.'

'She can wait,' he brushed aside her remark. 'At the moment you're more important.'

'Rick, I——' She swallowed convulsively as his fingers trailed a path of fire down her throat to where a little pulse beat out a furious rhythm. 'Please go now, and don't spoil the evening for yourself by worrying about me.'

His eyes flickered strangely, then he lowered his head and kissed her gently, but lingeringly until her soft lips quivered to life beneath his.

'Goodnight, Dale,' he murmured, an odd little smile hovering about his mouth, and moments later she was alone in her room with her heart drumming loudly in her ears.

She raised tentative fingers to her lips. She felt dazed and bewildered, but she was also afraid. She dared not let herself fall in love with Rick! Not *Rick!* He was thirty-five, he was her guardian, and he knew too much about the disastrous and humiliating circumstances of her birth. There was Melissa Arnell as well. What man would look at a girl like Dale when he could have someone as beautiful and unsoiled as Melissa Arnell?

Tears blurred her vision, but she wiped them away hastily. It was ridiculous to imagine she was in love with Rick. It was utterly and totally foolish, and it would be wiser not to dwell on the subject.

Life continued with a semblance of normality for Dale when she started classes at the college once more. The days and weeks sped by into the first week of September, and on the morning of her twentieth birthday she awoke with a feeling of nostalgia. Sister Teresa had always made it a special day by coming to her room first thing in the morning to wish her a happy birthday, but that was in the past. She was living with Rick and his mother now, and there was no earthly reason why they should be aware of the fact that it was a special day for her.

Brenda Crawford had, however, made it her business to find out somehow that it was Dale's birthday, and, at the breakfast table, she presented Dale with a box of the finest lace handkerchiefs, and an expensive blue silky scarf.

'I chose the colour to match your lovely eyes,' she smiled, and Dale hugged her impulsively when she thanked her.

Dale did not see Rick that morning, and she did not hear from him during the day. She felt vaguely disappointed, but she was too busy to let it trouble her, and the card from Sister Teresa which awaited her on her arrival home that afternoon more than made up for Rick's neglect.

She found him alone in the living-room when she went down to dinner that evening, and she hesitated in the doorway, reluctant to join him.

'Come here, Dale,' he instructed when he turned and saw her, and she obeyed him in abject silence. When she reached his side he swung her round so that she stood with her back to him, and only when she felt something cool against her skin did she realise that he was fastening a chain about her throat. It was a beautiful pendant with a single pearl set in a leaf design of gold, and she trembled unexpectedly when his warm fingers brushed against the nape of her neck. The small catch snapped into place, and then he was turning her to face him once more. 'Happy twentieth birthday.'

Overwhelmed, she fingered the pearl pendant and eyed him selfconsciously. 'I—I didn't think you—you knew.'

His mouth twitched as if in a smile. 'I have a file at the office which contains all the relevant details about you.'

'Oh!' she breathed foolishly, *and* a little unhappily when she was reminded of what that file contained.

'You seem shocked,' he commented.

'I'm a little surprised, that's all,' she laughed it away shakily. 'Silly of me, really, because as my guardian you would naturally have all the necessary information concerning me.'

His eyes narrowed perceptibly. 'I sometimes wish I knew more about you.'

'Oh?' she murmured, veiling her own eyes nervously.

'You're a rather mysterious young lady with eyes

that harbour dark secrets.' His mouth curved with a surprising sensuality. 'I find it quite intriguing.'

More than a little flustered, she recalled that she had not yet thanked him for her present, and she frantically grasped at this opportunity to change the subject. 'Thank you very much for this lovely birthday gift.'

'You could say it with a kiss, you know,' he mocked her.

Dale blushed profusely and, feeling like a gauche schoolgirl, she stood on tiptoe and kissed him lightly on his lean cheek.

Brenda Crawford walked into the living-room at that precise moment, and one sweeping glance was enough to take in Dale's embarrassment, the pearl pendant about her throat, and the wicked gleam in her son's eyes.

'I was wondering whether you would remember that it was Dale's birthday,' she said, casting a reproving glance in Rick's direction.

'I always remember birthdays, Mother,' he replied smoothly. 'You should know that.'

'Well, you certainly always seem to remember mine most annoyingly,' Brenda acknowledged with a wry humour.

It was a memorable evening, and one in which Dale could almost forget entirely the dark cloud which hovered in her past, but in time to come she was to be made painfully aware of the bitter legacy which life itself had bestowed upon her.

The year drew to a close, and Dale completed her secretarial course at the college. She was anxious to find herself employment, but Brenda insisted that she take a well-earned holiday before she applied for the posts which were being advertised. Christmas was once again a family affair, with Alex coming up from

Amanzimtoti for the occasion, and they spent those long, hot, but idyllic days cooling off in the pool, or simply lazing in the sun. Holidaymakers from all over the country made going down to the beach quite impossible, but no one missed Durban's golden stretch of sand while they could enjoy themselves in the lush, spacious grounds of Rick's home.

For Dale the year started explosively in more ways than one. Storm clouds gathered in the sky one afternoon towards the middle of January, and they darkened rapidly towards evening. The first heavy drops of rain fell shortly after eight that night, but two hours later it reached a peak that terrified Dale. She had always been nervous of thunderstorms, but this one simply scared her out of her wits. Lightning forked repeatedly across the night sky, crackling with electricity, and it was followed rapidly by a clap of thunder that made the earth tremble ominously.

The smell of sulphur permeated the air and, leaping up from her crouched position on the bed, Dale crossed the room to draw the curtains in the hope that she would feel less afraid, but when she reached the window the sky was suddenly lit up with a blinding flash that snaked down vertically to split a pine tree in half where it stood at the bottom end of the garden. She screamed without actually being aware of it, and it drowned out the earth-shattering clap of thunder which came simultaneously with the lightning. It seemed to go on for ever, and she was standing hunched against the wall beside the window with her hands pressed against her ears when her bedroom door was flung open to admit Rick.

'Dale, are you all right?' he asked anxiously, reaching her side in a few quick strides.

'Oh, Rick!' she cried hoarsely with a mixture of relief and terror, and she was shaking from head to foot as she literally leapt into his arms to bury her white, stricken face against his wide chest where she could feel the comforting heat of his body through his white shirt.

He held her for a moment against the hard length of his body, but when a mutinous, crackling roar in the night sky made her whimper and flinch violently, he lifted her in his arms as if she was no weight at all, and carried her towards the bed.

'Silly girl, why didn't you tell me you were afraid of thunderstorms?' he murmured, half sitting, half lying with her in his arms among the pillows on her bed. 'It's all right, don't tremble so. I'll stay with you until the storm is over.'

Burrowing her face into the hollow of his shoulder, she clutched at him a little wildly. 'I—I'm sorry, Rick, I—I don't usually mind the storms, but——'

'But this is a bad one, I know,' he finished for her, brushing her hair gently away from her face, and planting light, reassuring little kisses on her forehead and cheek when she started to cry softly. 'Hush now, it will soon be over.'

He held her like that for a long time with his cheek pressed against hers until her frightened shudders ceased, but the storm, which had abated outside, was now beginning to rage within her. She was all at once conscious of several disturbing factors; the flimsiness of her night attire, the muscled strength of Rick's arms about her, and the hardness of his male body into which she had curled herself so trustingly. She felt again that surging warmth inside her, pulsating through her, and this time she knew without doubt that she had done what she had fought against so desperately. She was in love with Rick, and with this knowledge an inexplicable need rose within her which was too strong to control. Reacting instinctively and without further thought, she turned her head so that her lips came to rest beneath his.

Dale's sheltered upbringing did not prepare her for what followed, but, loving Rick as she did, it did not frighten her. He kissed her gently at first, almost absently, but when her arms went up to circle his neck, his kiss deepened to become passionate and demanding, and she responded instantly, forgetting everything except the joy of this moment. The pressure of his lips parted hers, and he invaded her mouth with an intimacy that sent a shock of alien emotions coursing through her. His hands seemed to burn her skin through the silk of her robe as he crushed her small slenderness against him, and then he was caressing her with an intoxicating sensuality that awakened emotions which nothing, and no one had prepared her for.

Rick muttered something unintelligible as his fiery mouth raked along her throat, and Dale was too pleasantly aroused in mind and body to protest when his hand slid into the opening of her robe to cup her breast. A moan of pleasure escaped her, and a flame of desire shot through her which she could not yet fully understand. She knew a need to give of herself even though she did not quite know how, but she could not think coherently at that moment, and she willingly followed where Rick led her along this new, exciting path.

Words of love hovered on her lips, but they remained unspoken, and it saved her a great deal of humiliation some minutes later when she was plunged back to earth with a shattering jar from that ecstatic plane where she had been drifting so helplessly.

'For Pete's sake, what am I doing!' Rick barked hoarsely, dragging her arms from about his neck, and thrusting her away from him almost savagely as he swung his legs off the bed and stood up. He was breathing heavily as he stood there gazing down into her flushed, bewildered face, then his dark eyes filled with contempt. 'I must be going mad!'

Dale stared after him confusedly as he strode out of the room and closed the door firmly behind him. Her body was still hot and trembling with the emotions he had aroused, but her eyes became dark pools of pain in her white face as her mind slowly cleared.

She had invited his kisses unashamedly, and she could blame no one but herself for what had followed. Rick despised her, she had seen it in his eyes, and quite possibly he despised himself as well. He had allowed himself to be tempted into making love to his unattractive ward, but, more to the point, no man in his right mind wanted to become involved physically with a girl who was the illegitimate daughter of a madwoman.

It rained steadily outside, but the worst of the storm had passed. Dale, however, was battling against the odds of her own private storm. Rick had shown her quite clearly what to expect of the future, and her childish dreams of one day having a home and children of her own would have to be cast aside. If Rick, in his wisdom, could feel such utter contempt for her, then she could not expect anything other than rejection from anyone else.

CHAPTER FOUR

DALE saw very little of Rick during the weekend that followed, and when they did meet he was once again that cool, distant stranger she had met more than a year ago in the Mother Superior's office. She wanted desperately to talk to him, to explain, if possible, and apologise for her behaviour, but his unapproachable manner finally made her relinquish the idea.

'Master Rick wants to see you in his study, Miss Dale,' Lucy said one morning during the following week when she entered the breakfast room to clear away the dishes.

'Thank you, Lucy.'

Dale stared contemplatively at the cup of coffee in front of her, but a summons from Rick was not something to be ignored, and she knew only too well how impatient he could become if he was kept waiting. She paused only long enough to swallow down a mouthful, then she pushed her cup of coffee aside and got to her feet.

The study door stood open and Dale hovered nervously on the threshold when she saw Rick seated behind his desk, but he was studying an important-looking document in front of him, and was unaware of her presence until she knocked tentatively. He looked up at once, and his dark gaze flicked over her dispassionately.

'Come in, and close the door,' he ordered harshly, and she obeyed him in silence. He did not invite her to sit down, and she stood in front of his desk with her hands clasped behind her back like a child about to be reprimanded. Her eyes were lowered nervously, and her heart was pounding in her throat as she waited for his anger to wash over her, but she was totally unprepared for what followed. 'I've made arrangements for you to live with Alex. She needs a full-time secretary now that she's started her book, and she would prefer to have you rather than a stranger in her home.'

Dale looked up then, and her eyes were wide and incredulous. 'You—you're sending me away?'

'I'm not sending you away,' he explained with an intolerance that hurt. 'I've merely found you a job with Alex where I can still keep an eye on you until you come of age.'

Dale could have tolerated his anger, even his contempt, but this hurt more deeply than he would ever know, and her face went white beneath the golden tan she had acquired that summer.

'Rick, if—if this is because of what happened the other night, then I——'

'What happened the other night must never happen again!' he interrupted her with a harshness that made her flinch, and she backed away from him involuntarily.

'It was my fault, I——'

'It was no one's fault!' He rose to his feet, the look on his lean face forbidding her to continue. 'Circumstances led up to it, and I can't risk it happening again.'

She lowered her gaze and clenched her hands so tightly behind her back that her fingers ached. 'Does your mother know you've made arrangements for me to leave?'

'Yes, she knows.'

A tense, awkward silence settled between them before the anxious query was finally torn from her. 'Does she know why?'

His mouth tightened. 'I didn't consider it necessary

to enlighten her that I'd lost my head the other night with my ward.'

My ward. It was the first time she had heard him refer to her as such, and if she had still had any lingering hopes that he might care for her in some way, then those hopes were now totally dashed. She had been put firmly in her place. She was his ward; the unwanted responsibility which had been passed on from Ivan and Celeste Palmer to the nuns at St Stephen's, and finally to Rick. That was all that she would ever be—an unwanted, embarrassing responsibility!

Dale aged in that moment. She transcended from girlhood into womanhood before Rick's undiscerning eyes, and he would never know the pain he had caused when he had crushed the fragile bloom of her love beneath his careless feet.

'When—When did you want me to leave?' she finally asked in a quiet, halting voice.

'Alex wants you at Amanzimtoti as soon as possible.'

'I'll go upstairs and start packing.'

'Dale!' He was beside her in a flash, his strong fingers gripping her arm and preventing her from leaving. 'I'm doing this for your own good.'

She dared not look at him, she was not yet proficient in hiding her pain and the tears in her eyes and, nodding mutely, she disengaged her arm from his clasp and walked out of his study.

I must not cry, she told herself as she climbed up the stairs with her head erect on her slim, straight shoulders. She had nothing left except her pride, and she was not going to lay that at Rick's feet so that he could trample it as he had trampled on her love.

With Brenda Crawford's kind but unsuspecting help, Dale was packed and ready to leave after lunch that day. She did not see Rick again, and she was glad of that. Saying goodbye to him would have shattered her control, and she dared not risk that in front of his mother.

The drive down to Amanzimtoti took a little more than half an hour, but it was a hot afternoon, and the humidity was near unbearable.

'Am I glad to see you!' Alex exclaimed, ushering Dale into her cool, air-conditioned home while the servants took care of Dale's suitcases. 'My work is in such a mess that I'll never get it straightened out without the help of someone like yourself. I've been trying for weeks to get a decent secretary, but I simply never gave you a thought, and it was an absolute answer to my prayers when Rick called and asked if I wouldn't consider giving you the job as my secretary.' Alex laughed unexpectedly and hugged Dale. 'Listen to me babbling away! I'm so relieved and happy that you could come that I'm quite forgetting you must be dying of thirst!'

'I could do with a long, iced drink,' Dale confessed, lowering herself into a chair in the spacious living-room with its odd but attractive assortment of furniture ranging from antique to modern.

'What about a glass of iced lime?' Alex suggested, walking towards the table beside the window where a jug and glasses had been set out conveniently on a tray.

'Lovely,' Dale murmured, closing her eyes for a brief moment to ease the ache of unshed tears behind them. 'When do you want me to start work?'

'Most certainly not this afternoon,' Alex replied firmly when they both sat sipping their cool, refreshing drinks.

'Tomorrow?' Dale suggested, knowing that work was the only thing which would help her to come to terms with the future.

'I didn't want to sound like a slavedriver, so I'm

glad you suggested it,' Alex laughed a little self-consciously.

'I've been idle long enough over Christmas and New Year,' Dale replied gravely. 'I'm anxious now to start working.'

They talked for a while longer, discussing Dale's salary and working schedule, then Dale went up to her room, at Alex's suggestion, to rest before dinner.

Dale had little time to brood about herself during those first few days in Amanzimtoti. Working for Alex was unexpectedly interesting and exciting, and totally unlike what she had expected. There was also plenty of scope for the artist in Dale, and she spent her free time walking along the beach, sketching whatever caught her interest.

A little more than a week after Dale had arrived on Alex's doorstep, she walked into the study one morning to find Alex poring over a batch of photographs.

'Did you take these?' Dale asked, leaning over her shoulder to glance at the colourful array of photographs.

'Yes, but I can't possibly use them all,' Alex sighed ruefully. 'What I really need is someone who could do small illustrations of the foliage and the flowers for me.'

'I would like to try that, if you would let me,' Dale offered quietly, and dark eyes, so very like Rick's, were raised to study her speculatively.

'Well, I . . .'

'Sketching is a hobby of mine,' Dale confessed gravely, 'and if you don't like what I've done, then you can tell me so.'

A slow smile spread over Alex's attractive features, then she said excitedly, 'It's a deal!'

That evening after dinner, armed with photographs, sketch pad and an array of acrylic paints, Dale cleared a space in her room and erected her easel, then she began the intricate task she had set for herself. She worked steadily until after eleven before she went to bed, but she was up early the following morning to add the finishing touches.

Dale was pleased with the finished product, but the paint would take a while to dry before the three sketches would be ready for Alex's inspection, and that would not be before lunch.

Alex usually worked long hours into the night, perfecting her drafts before handing them over to Dale to be typed, but she nearly always took a break after lunch, and that left Dale with an hour to do as she pleased. On this particular afternoon Dale decided to go for a swim and, on her way out of the house, she left the sketches on Alex's desk.

The beach was not far from the house. Dale simply had to go out the side gate and take the steps down to the street. An alleyway between two blocks of flats gave her access to the beach-front, and with the holiday season at an end she practically had the entire stretch of sand and sea to herself.

She slipped out of her towelling robe and kicked off her sandals, leaving them on the sand beside her towel, then she ran down to the sea and plunged into the waves. The water was cool and refreshing, and she swam about lazily for some time before she realised that someone was surfing out with the waves alongside her. It was a young man of about her own age. He was wearing green briefs, and when he surfaced beside her his dark brown hair was plastered to his forehead. His muscled, youthful body was tanned a deep ochre, and his hazel eyes smiled into hers with an obvious attempt at making her acquaintance.

'Hello, I'm Tony Garrett,' he introduced himself, following her out of the surf and on to the sand where she had left her things. 'What's your name?'

'Dale Palmer,' she replied, deciding that he was not exactly the most attractive young man she had ever seen, but there was something nice about his smile and the way his eyes crinkled at the corners.

'Do you live here in Amanzimtoti, or are you on holiday?' he questioned her, leaving the sun to dry his body while she used her towel to dry her arms and legs.

'I live here,' she told him, then she gestured in the direction of Alex's house. 'Up there on the hill, as a matter of fact.'

He looked in the direction she had pointed, then he glanced back at her to ask incredulously, 'Mrs Murray's place?'

'Yes,' Dale said casually, wringing out her mousy-coloured hair and flicking it back over her shoulder. 'Do you know her?'

'Everyone knows Alexis Murray here in Amanzimtoti,' Tony announced. 'My father is crazy about her books, but I'm not so keen on travelogues and native customs, and things like that.' His eyes were narrowed against the sun as he studied her closely. 'Are you a relative of hers?'

'I work for her.'

'As her secretary, you mean?' he asked, offering her his hand to balance herself while she brushed the sand off her feet and slipped them into her sandals.

'That's right.'

'Is she writing another book?'

'On trees and shrubs of Natal, yes,' Dale replied, letting go of his hand and pulling on her robe.

'Just wait till I tell my father about that!' Tony smiled broadly. 'He'll never believe I've actually spoken to someone who knows her personally!'

'What do *you* do for a living?' she changed the subject.

'I'm a lifeguard here on the beach, but I'm also a

part-time insurance agent.' He noticed the determined way she tied the belt of her robe about her waist, and he actually looked a little distressed as she draped her towel over her arm. 'You're not going now, are you?'

'I have to get back to work.'

'But when am I going to see you again?'

Dale smiled for the first time, and she was quite unaware of the elusive, almost mysterious quality it added to her appearance. 'Perhaps tomorrow.'

'I shall look forward to it,' Tony told her, and raised his fingers to his forehead in a casual salute as they parted company.

Dale was in a thoughtful mood ten minutes later when she walked into Alex's luscious garden through the side gate. She was not quite sure whether she could afford to indulge in a friendship with that young man she had met on the beach. There was surely no harm in being friendly, was there? It would be safer, of course, to avoid any sort of relationship with men, but there was no sense in living like a recluse because of her dark heritage.

'Dale, is that you?' Alex called from the study when she heard Dale enter the house.

'Yes, Alex.'

'I've been looking at these sketches you left on my desk,' Alex said when Dale joined her. 'They're very good . . . in fact, they're *excellent*.'

'Do you think you could use them?' Dale asked, hesitant to accept Alex's praise.

'I not only think it, I *know* it,' Alex announced emphatically, and there was a definite gleam of excitement in her eyes when she added: 'Just wait till Newton Gould sees these sketches!'

Dale looked bewildered. 'Who's Newton Gould?'

'My publisher,' Alex smiled, clutching Dale's sketches in her hand. 'I'm expecting him here next week some time, and I'm simply dying for him to see your work.'

'You really think they're that good?' Dale asked, fingering the belt of her robe nervously.

'You'll find that, in some instances, Rick and I are alike,' Alex said, her eyes grave now as they met Dale's. 'We seldom if ever say things we don't mean. I think these sketches are excellent, and I think you have a definite talent, and I'll tell you something else . . .' She waved the sketches almost imperiously at Dale. 'If Newton Gould sees these and doesn't make you an offer of some sort, then I swear I'll never write another word!'

Dale did not reply to that, but accepted Alex's statement with more than a little scepticism. Newton Gould, whoever he was, must know hundreds of artists who could do whatever he wished. Why would he bother making an offer to someone who had never even had one single art lesson in all her life?

She went upstairs to shower and change, but there was no time to dry her hair, and it was still damp when she tied it back into its customary ponytail. She would have to do something about it, she realised at last as she went downstairs to join Alex in her study.

'I need to have my hair cut a little,' she remarked casually to Alex when they paused for tea that afternoon. 'Can you recommend a hairdresser here in Amanzimtoti?'

'I usually go to Damian's,' Alex replied, studying Dale contemplatively for a moment and, before she could protest, she had lifted the telephone receiver off its cradle and was dialling a number. 'I'll give Damian a call and make an appointment for you.'

Dale wished suddenly that she had kept her mouth shut, but it was too late now to do anything about it.

'Damian?' Alex was saying seconds later. 'I have a young friend here who's new to Toti. Do you think you could fit her in some time? . . . Dale Palmer . . . that will be perfect, thank you.' She replaced the receiver and smiled triumphantly at Dale. 'You have an appointment for nine o'clock on Friday morning, and you'll find Damian's salon in the shopping mall beyond the station.'

'Thank you,' Dale murmured somewhat agitatedly. 'I don't suppose I shall be away for more than an hour.'

'You may stay away as long as you like,' Alex told her. 'I'm giving you the day off.'

'That's very kind of you, Alex, but——'

'No "buts",' Alex interrupted sternly. 'You've worked hard these past two weeks, and you've earned a break.'

'You're spoiling me,' Dale protested, 'but thank you.'

Sheena, the Indian woman who had been Alex's cook and housekeeper for many years, came in to collect the tea tray, and after that there was no time to think of anything else except work.

Dale did not particularly want to go down to the beach the following afternoon to meet Tony Garrett, but she felt more or less under an obligation to do so, and perhaps he sensed her reluctance, for the first thing he said to her when they met was:

'I was wondering whether you'd come.'

'I only have enough time for a quick swim,' she warned, feeling a little guilty, but he nodded amiably.

'Suits me.'

Tony was a strong swimmer, but so was she, and she did not fall back when he swam beyond the swell of the breakers. The sea was reasonably calm that day, and when they drifted lazily on the swell, Tony explained how the shark nets worked along that stretch of the shoreline. Dale listened politely and questioned him intelligently, but she was becoming impatient to leave and, as soon as she could, she suggested swimming back to shore.

'Aren't you deserting your post by being here with me?' she asked him while she dried herself hurriedly and slipped her arms into her beach robe.

'It's quiet now, and I have someone watching the beach for me.' He stood tall and bronzed in the sun, the water dripping off his body on to the sand, and a frown appeared between his eyes when he realised that she was preparing to leave. 'Don't tell me you're going to rush off straight away?'

'I did warn you that I only had time for a quick swim, and now I have to get back to work.'

'What about the weekend?' he asked, falling into step beside her and walking a little distance of the way.

'I can't promise anything.'

He touched her arm lightly, forcing her to pause and turn to face him. 'Do you know where the beach office is?'

'Yes.'

'I'll be there all Saturday afternoon, if you can make it.'

Dale nodded, but felt compelled to say, 'If you find something better to do, then don't put it off for my sake.'

He grinned boyishly and, saluting her as he had done the day before, he walked briskly away from her across the hot sand.

Dale found the salon without difficulty, but she felt a little wary when she read the painted sign at the entrance. *Damian's—Beauticians and Hair Stylists.* It looked expensive and not what she had wanted at all, but she would not get an appointment elsewhere at such short notice, and if she went home without having her hair trimmed, then Alex might be annoyed at having gone to all this trouble for nothing on her behalf.

She pushed open the door and stepped into the perfumed interior, and her helpless sigh became strangled in her throat. Women were paging idly through magazines as they sat under the driers, and others languished in partitioned cubicles for a manicure while their hair was being styled by uniformed girls who obviously knew what they were doing. The pink, white, and gold elegance of the place made Dale want to rush outside again, but at that precise moment she was looking into the enquiring eyes of the girl behind the reception desk. She gave her name, and was instantly ushered into a cubicle where she was left to sit staring at her reflection in the mirror.

She looked like a scared, grey little fieldmouse which had accidentally ventured into a cage of hungry cats, and she only just had time to pull herself together when the curtain behind her was swept aside. A man of medium height, slim and about forty, stepped into the cubicle. He was dressed in white, with dark hair curling about his ears, and the light above the mirror glinted on a heavy gold chain dangling from his neck.

'Good morning, I'm Damian,' he smiled, inclining his head gallantly at her mirror image. 'And you are?'

She looked up into keen, dark eyes, and tried to place that slight continental accent as she said: 'Dale Palmer.'

'Ah, Dale ... valley ... deep ... mysterious.' He slowly, and embarrassingly waded through the association of words. 'I see it all in your eyes ... your mouth ...'

'Do you think you could trim my hair a little? It's grown rather uncomfortably long,' she hastily voiced the reason for her presence there in his salon.

'My little sparrow,' he gestured expressively, and an amused smile curved his wide, sensual mouth. 'When

I am done with you, you will look like a sleek, glossy starling.'

Dale was not too sure what he was talking about, and she wondered whether this was his usual line of patter to his clients. She let it pass, however, and subjected herself to a shampoo by the expert himself.

'Your hair is much too long. It should reach no further than here,' he said, tapping her shoulder with a slender finger. 'I am going to cut it and style it in a way which will be easy for you to manage on your own.'

'But I like my hair long,' she protested almost indignantly.

'I know you do, my little sparrow,' he replied gravely, 'but I beg of you to trust my judgment.'

Dale hesitated, then she thought, 'Why not?' She stared at her image in the mirror and, before she could change her mind, she said: 'Very well, do as you wish.'

Armed with scissors and comb, Damian snipped away, and she watched with grave trepidation as long strands of hair fell to the floor. What, she wondered, would Sister Teresa have said about this?

Using no more than a hand drier and a hot brush, he finally styled her hair so that it curled softly about her head, giving her face a slightly fuller appearance.

'Now tell me,' he said, stepping away from her so that she could appraise herself in the mirror, 'does that not look magnificent?'

'My hair looks fairer ... brighter somehow,' she admitted, taking in the unexpected golden sheen, then the glanced up at him warily. 'I hope you didn't colour it?'

'I used the correct shampoo for your hair,' he smiled, handing her the empty bottle so that she could read the trade name. 'It has been created to bring out the natural colour and gloss in the hair.'

Dale placed the bottle on the shelf in front of her and started to rise from the chair. 'Thank you very much.'

'Sit down, my little sparrow,' he instructed, taking her lightly by the shoulders and pushing her back into the chair with that now familiar, amused smile hovering about his mouth. 'You are only half way to becoming a starling.'

Her hands fluttered a little nervously in her lap. 'I—I don't know what you mean?'

'I am going to give you a facial,' he announced.

'Oh, but I——'

'Do you want to be a sparrow for ever?' he demanded. 'Or will you trust my judgment once again and walk out of here a glossy starling?'

Apart from the sparrow and starling nonsense, he had done a good job on her hair, but she eyed him dubiously for a moment. 'Tell me first what you have in mind.'

'First,' he said, studying her critically, 'you have a good, healthy skin, and I'm going to show you how to take care of it. Second, you have lovely, secretive eyes, and a sensitive, passionate mouth. With the correct application of a little make-up we will create a different *you*.'

Embarrassed by his observations, Dale said a little sharply, 'I never use make-up.'

'I assure you that it will not hurt,' he smiled, 'and I shall use very little, but it will make all the difference in the world.'

Dale could not suppress the faintly cynical smile that curved her mouth. 'Why do I have this feeling that you're attempting to make me look attractive?'

'But you *are* attractive!' Damian insisted, gesturing characteristically. 'You have good bone structure, and good teeth, and the eyes of a Madonna with hidden depths. Your face has character, and that, my little sparrow, is more attractive than a pretty face on the page of a glossy magazine.'

'Are you an amateur psychologist as well as a beautician?' she asked drily, amusement lurking in her eyes, and Damian smiled back at her.

'You are laughing at me, and that is a good sign that you possess a sense of humour,' he said. 'I admit that at times I flatter my clients, but then they are perhaps not so young, and in need of flattery. You, my little sparrow, are still young, and the bloom of youth is still on your cheeks. There is no need to flatter you, only to speak the truth, and that is what I have done.'

Dale relaxed in the chair, but she could not help feeling sceptical about the whole thing. 'I shall try very hard to believe you.'

'There is no need to say more,' he assured her. 'You may give me your opinion when I have done with you.'

Damian tilted her chair back and proceeded to give her a facial which not only treated her skin, but seemed to relax every muscle in her face. He talked softly while he worked, telling her what creams and lotions to use for the preservation of her skin, and when he finally applied the make-up he followed the same procedure. He explained what he was using, and how to apply it. Only when he was completely satisfied did he stand aside for her to see herself in the mirror, and it felt to her as if she were looking at a stranger.

The natural arch of her eyebrows had been left untouched, while a subtle touch of eye-shadow and mascara enhanced the beauty of her deep blue eyes, and naturally long lashes. He had used a light base beneath the dusting of powder, and a shell-pink lipstick accentuated the attractive curve of her lips. She was not beautiful, not by Melissa Arnell's standards, but as she studied herself critically for the first time in her life, she knew that never again would she think of herself as unattractive.

'Well?' Damian smiled at her image in the mirror.

'I—I can't believe what I'm seeing,' she whispered, gesturing helplessly with her hands.

'You are satisfied now that I spoke the truth?'

'I'm satisfied,' she answered gravely, 'and I don't know how to thank you.'

'You may thank me by remembering everything I have told you,' Damian smiled and, taking her hand, he raised it to his lips. 'I have given you a new image, but the irresistible mystery is still there and, together, it is a striking combination.'

Dale left Damian's with the odd feeling that she had begun a new life, but the old life was still there to haunt her. She posted the letter she had written with such care the previous evening, and only then did she do her shopping and stop for lunch.

It was late that afternoon before she returned home, and she found Alex on the terrace with a wad of notes on her lap, and a tall glass of iced lime on the table beside her.

'Dale!' the older woman exclaimed when she looked up suddenly, and her surprised expression was swiftly replaced by a look of approval. 'I always knew that with a little encouragement you could make yourself look extremely attractive!'

The truth suddenly hit Dale. 'You sent me to Damian on purpose!'

'Am I forgiven?' Alex smiled apologetically.

'I feel so good at the moment that I'll forgive you anything, Alex,' Dale sighed happily, lowering herself into the nearest chair.

'By the way,' said Alex, putting aside her notes, 'Rick telephoned to say that Mother is driving down tomorrow morning to spend the weekend with us.'

'Oh, but that's wonderful!' Dale smiled, her eyes becoming misty. 'I've missed her.'

'And Rick?' Alex asked, studying her intently. 'Have you missed him too?'

Dale looked away, carefully controlling her expression as she absently fingered her parcels. 'Yes, I've missed him.'

'He asked how you were, and sent his apologies,' Alex continued. 'He would have liked to come down this weekend with Mother, but he's going to be very busy these next few weeks, and he'll most probably have to work this weekend.'

'I met someone the other day whose father is a fan of yours,' Dale changed the subject.

'Oh?'

'His name is Tony Garrett, and he's a lifeguard on the beach, but his father is the one who's so crazy about your books,' Dale explained.

'You should invite this young man home one evening.'

'I don't think so,' Dale declined hastily. 'We've only met twice, and he works as an insurance agent in the evenings.'

She felt Alex's curious expression resting on her, and decided to take her parcels up to her room before she found herself having to answer awkward questions. Tony Garrett was not a friend, but simply an acquaintance, and she did not want Alex to think that there was something special developing between them. She remembered suddenly that Tony had invited her to meet him at the lifeguards' office the following afternoon, but, with Brenda Crawford coming for the weekend, she had no intention of keeping that appointment.

CHAPTER FIVE

THE weekend passed much too swiftly, and it felt to Dale as if Mrs Crawford had hardly arrived before it was time for her to leave again.

'I hope that next time Rick will accompany me,' was the last thing Brenda said before she left the Sunday afternoon, and Dale secretly wished the same. She missed Rick; she missed him more than she had thought possible, but she dared not let anyone suspect her feelings.

The week ahead promised to be a busy one, but Newton Gould's arrival on the Wednesday halted everything almost for the entire morning. He was a man of about forty-five with a vital, bracing manner, and his enthusiasm matched Alex's when he studied the sketches Dale had made.

'Have you had any training in art, young lady?' he questioned Dale.

'None at all.'

'Remarkable,' he murmured and, before his departure later that morning, he paused beside Dale's desk to say, 'You'll be hearing from me.'

There was nothing idle about his remark, Dale gathered later from Alex. Newton Gould never made rash promises, and Dale would be assured of a bright future in his publishing company the moment her job with Alex was completed. Dale was not quite sure that this was what she wanted, but for the moment it was enough to know that what she now considered a hobby might one day become a profitable occupation.

She did not have the opportunity to go down to the beach again until the following Sunday morning. She was lying basking in the sun after her leisurely swim when she felt someone trickle sand on to her back. She raised her head sharply to see Tony Garrett smiling down at her, and it was so infectious that she found herself smiling back at him.

'I waited for you last Saturday,' he accused, stretching himself out on the sand beside her.

'I'm sorry, but I couldn't make it.'

'Don't tell me you work weekends as well?'

'No,' she shook her head and pushed herself up on to her elbows. 'Mrs Murray's mother came down for the weekend, and——'

'And you had to play nursemaid,' he filled in incorrectly.

'Oh, no, it isn't like that at all,' she contradicted hastily. 'I had been living with Mrs Crawford for the past year, and I'm extremely fond of her.'

'Were you the old lady's secretary?' Tony probed, slanting a curious glance at her.

'No, I . . .' She paused uncomfortably, but decided that the truth would not hurt. 'Mrs Crawford's son is an attorney, and he's also my guardian until I turn twenty-one.'

His hazel eyes sharpened with interest. 'Your parents are dead?'

'Yes,' she replied, her expression clouding.

'I'm sorry,' he said, and he seemed to mean it. 'My mother died when I was five, and since then it's only been my dad and me.' He studied Dale a little more closely, sliding his glance over her slim body as if he were searching for something. 'You know, there's something different about you.'

'I've had my hair cut,' she smiled, watching his brow clear, and they talked for some time after that until she pulled on her shorts and T-shirt, and pushed her feet into her sandals. 'I must go, Tony,' she said, slapping her cloth hat against her thigh to get the sand out of it before she rammed it on to her head.

'You look like a little girl,' Tony smiled, looking her up and down. 'All you need now is a bucket and a spade, then you're set to build sandcastles!'

'Thanks!' she replied, pretending to be indignant.

'When will I see you again?'

'Perhaps next week some time,' she promised vaguely. 'I can't make any definite arrangements.'

'I'll settle for that,' he grinned, and after that they parted company.

Dale walked home at a leisurely pace. There was no hurry, and it was such a lovely day that she could quite easily have stayed out on the beach all afternoon as well, but Alex was expecting her home for lunch.

. A little breathless after climbing the forty or more steps, she pushed open the side gate and entered the shady garden. She took her time strolling up to the house, enjoying the birdsong in the trees, but something, a movement perhaps, made her glance towards the steps leading on to the terrace, and then the most incredible joy surged through her. Rick was standing there, and her heart hammered wildly against her ribs at the sight of his tall, lean and vital frame in grey lightweight pants and jacket. His dark eyes were appraising her intently as she approached him, and it was with the greatest difficulty that she prevented herself from rushing headlong into his arms.

'Surprised to see me?' he asked when she reached the bottom step and stood looking up at him, and she saw his glance linger for a moment on her slim, shapely legs.

'I—I wasn't expecting you,' her voice faltered with nervous excitement.

She could barely take her eyes off him, almost like someone quenching a terrible thirst. She had tried not to think of him during these weeks she had been at Amanzimtoti, but seeing him again made her realise precisely how much she had missed this formidable, often stern man. But her joy became slightly soured the next moment when Melissa Arnell stepped out on to the terrace to join them, and her beauty once again aroused that familiar awkwardness in Dale.

'Well, what have we here?' Melissa smiled coldly into Dale's eyes. 'Did you come back for your bucket and your spade, darling?'

Dale had found it amusing when Tony had passed a similar remark, but from Melissa Arnell it was an obvious insult, and the laughter in Rick's eyes simply added to her chagrin.

'If you'll excuse me I'll go up and change,' she said coldly and, brushing past them, she entered the house and went up to her room.

She was so angry that she was shaking when she reached the seclusion of her bedroom. Why did Rick have to invite Melissa to join him on this visit? Did he bring her with him for the purpose of making sure Dale understood that she could never be anything more than his *ward*? Dear heaven! Rick was so far beyond her reach, and had he not made it quite plain that, other than his responsibility towards her, he felt nothing but contempt for her?

Dale stepped into the shower and opened the taps until the water beat hard against her body. She stood like that for some time until her anger and despair were thrashed out of her, and only then did she soap her body and shampoo her hair. She felt refreshed and considerably calmer after her shower and, with her towel draped sarong style around her body, she walked barefoot into her bedroom. From her wardrobe she selected a sky blue silk dress which was her favourite. It made her feel and look good, and she needed the latter desperately.

Half an hour later she went downstairs, but the sound of Melissa's voice in the living-room made Dale change direction abruptly to enter Alex's study. She could not face that woman yet, not until she was totally composed, she decided as she opened the study door and stepped inside, but the next instant she caught her breath sharply. The study was not empty. Rick was there, and he was studying the sketches she had completed for Alex's book. He looked up when she entered, and his eyes met hers only briefly before they slid down the length of her and back again to her face. His razor-sharp glance did not miss the difference in her appearance, but his features remained immobile, and Dale's legs suddenly felt as if they had turned to jelly. She waited, too afraid almost to move, but the topic he chose to discuss with her at that moment had absolutely nothing to do with the way she looked.

'Alex tells me you're doing the illustrations for her book.'

'Yes, she—she seems to think they're good,' Dale stammered foolishly, stepping a little further into the room.

'Her publisher also appears to think that they're worth something,' Rick added tersely and, when Dale nodded, he said accusingly, 'You never told me you were interested in art.'

'You never asked me,' she replied calmly as she slowly regained her composure.

'I'd thought we'd reached the stage where you could speak freely to me without being prodded for information.'

He sounded impatient and displeased and, as always, it had the power to hurt her. 'Sketching has always been a hobby and a source of amusement to me. I've never considered it worth mentioning, but neither have I hidden it. Your mother, for instance, has known about it for a long time.'

Rick digested this for a moment, then he rapped out a question. 'If Gould makes you an offer, are you going to accept it?'

'*If* is the operative word,' she smiled wryly. 'He hasn't made me an offer yet, and if he does then I might consider it.'

Rick dropped the sketches on to Alex's desk, and studied Dale intently as he thrust his hands deep into the pockets of his pants. 'You've changed these past weeks.'

'Have I?' she asked cautiously, observing him through lowered lashes.

'You're exceedingly calm and poised, and very aloof.' His mouth twisted into a semblance of a smile. 'I'm not sure that I approve of the way you are now.'

'I haven't really changed,' she argued quietly.

'Perhaps not,' he shrugged, crossing the room towards her, and her heartbeat quickened when he stood directly in front of her. He raised a hand, and brushed his knuckles lightly against her cheek in that familiar caress, but this time his touch felt like fire against her skin. 'Don't change too much,' he warned in a deep, strangely vibrant voice. 'And don't drift too far away.'

Dale frowned. 'I don't know what you mean.'

The door opened behind them before he could reply, and the breeze from the terrace caused a draught through the hall so that Melissa's perfume preceded her into the study.

'I've been looking everywhere for you, darling,' she smiled, sliding a possessive arm through Rick's. 'Alex is waiting out on the terrace for us.'

'Alex will have to wait a while longer.'

'Aren't you coming now?' Melissa pouted persuasively.

'I have something to discuss with Dale.'

Melissa glanced at Dale for the first time since entering the study, and there was no pretence of warmth in her eyes now as they met Dale's, only an

icy venom which Dale finally understood. Melissa had
tolerated her presence as Rick's 'pathetically plain'
ward, but, with the help of Damian's artistry and
advice, Melissa was beginning to see her as a threat.
Her entire attitude suddenly said: 'Rick is mine!
Hands off!' And Dale smiled inwardly, for Melissa
had, unknowingly, given her the most wanted gift—
confidence in herself!

'Well, don't be too long, will you?' Melissa was
saying sweetly, but the smile she cast in Dale's
direction was clearly threatening as she swept out of
the study and closed the door behind her.

Dale felt a little shaken by Melissa's manner, but
Rick appeared to be unperturbed as he seated himself
on the corner of Alex's desk.

'You'll be twenty-one in a few months from now,
and as the main shareholder of your late father's
company you will have the right to sit in on their
meetings.' Rick held her glance effortlessly with his
compelling eyes. 'Have you given this matter a
thought at all?'

'No, I haven't,' she replied with inherent honesty.
'Do I have to take an active part in these decision-
making meetings?'

'You don't have to, but then I would suggest that
you think about appointing someone who could take
care of your interests in that respect.'

'You've been doing that for me since my—my father
died,' she pointed out hesitantly, not quite sure what
this conversation was leading up to.

'That's correct,' Rick acknowledged tersely, 'but
when you're twenty-one you'll have the right to select
someone of your own choice.'

'I can't think of anyone else but you,' she told him
without giving the matter further thought, but when
she noticed the frown between his dark brows she
wondered whether he was perhaps finding the task too

irksome. 'Would it be expecting too much of you to hope that you would continue seeing to the business side of my affairs?'

His eyebrows rose mockingly. 'Do you trust me?'

'I can't think of anyone I could trust more,' she confessed, and he nodded abruptly.

'I appreciate that, and I accept provisionally, but there's still plenty of time for you to change your mind, and I want you to give this matter considerable thought during the next few months,' he instructed, then he changed the subject abruptly. 'Are you happy here?'

The swiftness with which he switched from one thing to the other nearly always succeeded in wrenching the truth from her, but on this occasion she bit back the revealing reply that she had missed him, and simply said: 'I've been very happy.'

'I believe you've met a young man on the beach.' He observed her intently. 'How serious is it?'

'I've only met him a few times, and I have no intention of letting it develop into something serious,' she answered tritely.

'Take care whom you confide in, Dale,' Rick warned. 'You're a wealthy young girl, and some men would do anything for money.'

Dale felt annoyed that he could even suggest such a thing about Tony Garrett and, turning from him abruptly, she snapped, 'I can take care of myself, thank you.'

'Dale!' His voice was harsh, but his hands were even harsher on her shoulders as he swung her round to face him, and his action brought her so close to him that she could feel the bone-melting heat of his body against her own. Contrary to her wishes she found herself recalling that night she had lain in his arms during the storm, and the desire to feel his arms about her once again was so strong that her breath quickened, parting her lips in an unconscious invitation. She was drowning in his smouldering eyes as he lowered his head towards hers, but before their lips could touch Rick was thrusting her from him, and saying abruptly, 'We'd better join the others on the terrace.'

She saw again the contempt in his eyes as he opened the door and stood aside for her to precede him and, cut to the core, she vowed silently that no man would ever have cause to look at her again with contempt in his eyes. She had forgotten for one brief moment that her unsavoury heritage would always stand between her and happiness, but she would not forget again.

The day passed without further incident, but Dale was intensely relieved when Rick and Melissa returned to Durban later that afternoon, and Alex seemed to harbour the same feelings.

'I hope Rick knows what he's letting himself in for if he decides to marry that woman,' was all she said, and from that Dale gathered that Alex was not too fond of the beautiful Melissa Arnell.

'I'm not happy with my drafts, so I haven't much typing for you to do today,' said Alex at the breakfast table a few weeks later. 'What I do need are some sketches of the small aloes which grow farther down on the south side of the beach.'

'I'll pack my sketchbook and pencils and go down there,' Dale agreed at once.

'Take a beach umbrella with you,' Alex suggested. 'It's going to be a scorcher today by the looks of it, and if you like I'll get Sheena to prepare a few sandwiches and a flask of coffee for lunch, then you won't have to rush back.'

'That would be nice,' Dale agreed, finishing her coffee and excusing herself from the table to pack her small rucksack and change into shorts and a thin sweater.

An hour later she was walking along the stretch of beach towards Doonside, and when she found what she was searching for she set up the umbrella. She pulled the brim of her cloth hat over her eyes to shade them from the glare of the sun, then she unpacked her rucksack and settled down to work. This was the most enjoyable part of her job. She could sketch all day without tiring, and while she worked she found herself considering for the first time an artistic career. It might not be a very remunerative occupation, but that did not really matter. She would have a steady income, Ivan Palmer had seen to that, and what more did she really want except a small place of her own to work and live in.

The morning passed swiftly, and she was beginning to think of stopping for lunch when a shadow fell across her sketch pad. Startled, she looked up into the rugged face of a man whose age she guessed to be close to fifty, and saw that his hazel eyes were fixed intently on the sketchpad resting on her knee.

'I see you're sketching the aloes,' his deep, quiet voice remarked. 'They're lovely, aren't they?'

'Lovely,' she agreed, not quite sure what to make of this man in his baggy khaki pants and white, open-necked shirt that appeared to be a size too small to accommodate the width of his shoulders.

'I can't sketch the aloes, so the next best thing is snapping them with my camera,' he smiled, gesturing towards the expensive-looking camera which was slung about his neck. 'Would it disturb you if I sat here for a while and watched you?'

He looked harmless, she decided and, eyeing him from beneath the brim of her cloth hat, she said: 'It wouldn't disturb me at all.'

She worked on, her pencil moving rapidly across the paper, and almost forgot about the man seated beside her on the sand until he lit his pipe and the pleasant aroma of his tobacco drifted towards her.

'My name is Joseph, by the way—Joseph Garrett,' he introduced himself eventually, and his eyes laughed into hers. 'My friends call me Joe.'

Dale studied him thoughtfully for a moment. 'You wouldn't, by any chance, have a son called Tony?'

'That's right,' he nodded, his eyes narrowed against the sun as he observed her questioningly.

'I'm Dale Palmer,' she enlightened him. 'Perhaps Tony has told you that we've met a few times on the beach?'

'Good heavens, yes,' he laughed softly, his brow clearing. 'You're Alexis Murray's secretary.'

'Secretary and illustrator,' Dale replied with a hint of pride in her voice. 'That's why I'm here sketching the aloes.'

'Do you know that I have every single book she's written about South Africa?' He gestured expressively with his pipe. 'She makes everything sound so fascinating that I find myself looking at my country with renewed interest.'

For a moment only the sound of the surf disturbed the silence, then she said impulsively, 'Perhaps you would like to meet her some time?'

His kindly, craggy face creased into a smile. 'I would consider it a great honour.'

'I have a flask of coffee here, and a batch of sandwiches large enough to feed six,' she told him. 'Would you care to share my lunch with me?'

'I should really be going home,' he told her, but he changed his mind when he saw her unpacking her lunch. 'Those sandwiches are much too tempting to resist!'

Dale poured coffee into the cap of the flask for herself, and used the mug Sheena had given her for Joe Garrett.

'I own a construction company in Durban, but the business more or less runs itself, and that gives me plenty of time to indulge in my hobby,' he said, gesturing towards his camera once again while they ate the ham and tomato sandwiches. 'I travel quite a bit too.'

'Alex travels a great deal too when she's researching a book,' Dale informed him, biting into her second sandwich.

'How very interesting.'

She studied him thoughtfully while they finished their meal in silence. Tony resembled his father slightly, it was something about the eyes and the mouth, and the way he smiled. Joe Garrett seemed gentle and nice, yet strong and dependable, and she felt certain that Alex would find him an interesting companion.

'Amanzimtoti is such a small place it seems strange to think that you and Alex have never met each other,' she remarked at length.

'There was a time when we might have met,' he confessed, draining his mug and putting it down beside him on the sand. 'I'd been invited to a small function where she was to be the guest speaker, but I picked up a bug on one of my travels and couldn't make it.'

'What a shame,' Dale murmured sympathetically. 'Is your telephone number in the book?'

'Yes,' he nodded, glancing at her strangely.

'I'll see what I can arrange, and I'll give you a call.'

A flicker of surprise lit his eyes. 'Would you really do that?'

'I'm sure Alex would be delighted to meet someone who's so interested in her books,' Dale replied with conviction.

'I shall be waiting anxiously to hear from you, then,' he smiled and, dusting the crumbs off his pants, he got to his feet. 'Well, I must go, but it's been delightful chatting to you, and thank you for sharing your lunch with me. I hope to return the compliment some day.'

Dale watched him walk away across the sandy beach, his strides long and leisurely, then she picked up her sketchbook and pencil and concentrated on her work once more.

From the tip of her charcoal pencil the spiky leaves of the aloes emerged on the paper. Coloured pencils filled in the dull green, and later it would be reproduced in oils instead of the acrylics she had used on the original sketches she had made for Alex. The aloes would not flower before July, which was a pity, Dale thought, but Alex had enough photographs from which she could work.

It was after five that afternoon before Dale arrived back at the house, and she went at once to the study to produce the sketches for Alex's approval.

'Hm, this is good,' Alex announced enthusiastically, trying to decide which of the four sketches she preferred.

'I met Tony Garrett's father on the beach,' Dale told her. 'Do you remember I told you about the man who's such a fan of yours?'

'I remember,' Alex replied absently.

'He's extremely nice, and he's dying to meet you.'

'Is he?'

'I have a feeling you're not really listening to me,' Dale accused.

'I'm listening,' Alex sighed, putting the sketches down and smiling faintly as she leaned back in her chair.

'May I invite him over one evening?'

Alex seemed to hesitate, but the smile about her lovely mouth deepened the next instant. 'If you do invite him, then please make it a Friday evening, and you may as well extend a similar invitation to his son. Between the four of us we will, I hope, keep the conversation flowing.'

'Thank you,' Dale smiled, feeling pleased with herself for some reason as she turned towards the door.

'Before you go, Dale, here's a letter for you from the Department of the Interior,' Alex said, mischief lurking in her eyes as she handed Dale the letter. 'Did you lose your identity documents?'

Dale felt curiously sick inside as she fingered the official-looking envelope. 'No . . . oh, no, I——'

'What is it, Dale?' Alex interrupted anxiously, getting up from her chair to place a hand on Dale's shoulder. 'You're shaking!'

'I—I'm all right,' Dale lied.

'Are you afraid of something you might find in that letter?' Alex demanded with surprising shrewdness, and Dale knew then that she could no longer bear the burden of her problem alone.

'Alex, I—I have to talk to someone, and I simply can't discuss this with Rick.'

'Is it that serious?' Alex wanted to know, and Dale nodded miserably.

'I wrote to the Department of the Interior hoping that they might be able to give me some information about my father.'

'Your father?' Alex seemed startled, and her hand fell away from Dale's shoulder. 'But surely you know all there is to know about your parents?'

'I'm talking about my *real* father.'

'Your *real* father?' Alex echoed uncharacteristically, and a strange whiteness settled about her mouth, but Dale attached no special significance to it at that precise moment.

'Ivan and Celeste Palmer adopted me when my mother died,' Dale explained. 'Ivan's sister, Emily, was my real mother.'

'Who told you that Ivan and Celeste were not your real parents?' Alex demanded sharply, and Dale lowered her eyes guiltily.

'No one told me, I—I found out quite by accident.'

'How?' Alex questioned abruptly, her manner very much like Rick's at that moment.

'Your mother sent me to get envelopes in Rick's desk one day, and I happened to see a letter addressed to Rick in my father's handwriting,' the truth was torn from her.

'And you read it?'

'It was wrong of me, I know, but I did,' Dale confessed, biting her lip.

'And in this letter Ivan mentioned that you were his sister's child?' Alex probed, her eyes intent on Dale's white, pinched face.

'Her *illegitimate* child,' Dale corrected distastefully.

'Oh, my goodness!' Alex passed a shaky hand over her face, and turned slowly towards the window which overlooked the garden. 'Perhaps you'd better open that letter and see what it says.'

Dale obeyed and ripped off the end of the envelope to extract a single sheet of paper with the department's stamp beneath the scribbled signature. She read through it quickly, and looked up to meet Alex's questioning, vaguely anxious glance.

'It says briefly that they have no records giving the name of the father of Emily Palmer's child,' Dale told her, and disappointment was rife in her voice.

'I suggest you leave the matter there,' Alex instructed, thrusting her hands into the pockets of her wide skirt.

'I can't!' Dale cried, crushing the letter in her trembling hands. 'There are certain things I must know—important things—and only *he* can tell me!'

'What important things?' Alex questioned with a guarded look in her eyes which Dale could not fathom.

'I—I can't tell you about it, but I must find my real father and talk to him,' Dale whispered miserably, then she raised imploring eyes to the woman facing

her. 'Alex, where do I go from here? Please help me
. . . tell me where to start my search?'

Alex's face went a shade whiter, and her eyes
suddenly acquired a haunted look as if she were
fighting her own private battle. For several seconds
only the sound of the flamboyant tree's branches
scraping against the window could be heard, then Alex
visibly squared her shoulders.

'You'll be wasting your time,' she announced
fatalistically.

'But I have to try,' Dale insisted. 'It's important!'

'Your father is dead, Dale,' Alex told her bluntly.
'He's been dead for almost nineteen years.'

'*Dead?*' Dale echoed in a croaky voice as she saw
her last hope of learning the truth disintegrating
before her eyes, but a measure of disbelief remained.
'How do you know he's dead?'

'Your father left Durban before you were born, and
went to Johannesburg,' Alex astonished Dale with her
knowledge. 'He was a heavy drinker and seldom
managed to stay sober for more than a week at a time.
He caught a chill during one of his drinking bouts, and
it was during his stay in hospital that they discovered
he was rotten with tuberculosis. He died shortly after
that.'

'*How do you know?*' Dale repeated her question a
little more frantically now.

Pain darkened Alex's eyes and etched deep lines
about her mouth. 'Your father was Nigel Murray . . .
my husband.'

The room spun crazily about Dale, and she felt
around blindly for a chair, but when she found none
she leaned heavily against the desk, and stared at Alex
incredulously.

'Nigel Murray was my father?'

'Yes.'

'You've known this all the time?'

'Yes, my dear, but——'

'And you never hated me?' Dale asked in a hoarse, incredulous whisper.

'Why should I hate you, Dale?' Alex seemed to come alive, and crossed the room hastily to Dale's side. 'I never hated your mother at the time. I felt deeply sorry for her, because she'd been duped by Nigel as much as I had been.'

The most awful thought leapt into Dale's mind and spilled from her lips. 'Did—Did my mother know he was married when—when——'

'She didn't know,' Alex interrupted her faltering query with understanding. 'I heard afterwards that Nigel had kept her dangling on a string until a month before you were born, and only then did he tell her that he couldn't marry her because he was already married . . . to me.'

'And poor Emily's fragile mind snapped,' Dale added to herself when Alex's explanation, given without malice, came to an end.

'Dear heaven!' Dale breathed, lifting her hand to her throat in an attempt to ease away the tightness. 'Does Rick know about this? And your mother?'

'They know,' Alex confirmed gently. 'My father was Ivan's attorney, remember, and Rick took over after my father's death.'

'Yes, of course,' Dale muttered, angry with herself for asking such a stupid question.

'Dale . . .' Alex placed a light, comforting hand on her shoulder. 'Forget the past.'

'I wish I could,' Dale sighed unhappily, 'but the past has so much bearing on the future.'

'I know your childhood was not a very happy one, and that Ivan could have given you a proper home instead of simply his name,' Alex remarked with a puzzled frown. 'What else is there that's troubling you?'

'What do you know about my mother?' Dale risked the question which had taken priority in her tortured mind.

'I know nothing about her except that she died a few weeks after giving birth to you.' Alex studied Dale's pale features closely. 'What in particular did you want to know?'

'It doesn't matter,' Dale hastily brushed aside the subject.

'Dale?'

'There's one other thing.' Dale's eyes were wide and anxious as they met Alex's. 'May I trust you not to mention this matter to Rick?'

'I was going to suggest that you talk to him. He's really the only one who might be able to fill in the details for you.'

Rick might have the information Dale needed so desperately, but, loving him as much as she did, he was the one man on this earth whom she could not confront with her problem.

'That won't be necessary,' Dale shook her head firmly. 'I think I will take your advice and forget the past after all.'

'Perhaps that's the wisest decision,' Alex agreed quietly. 'And you have my word that I shan't mention any of this to Rick.'

Dale kissed her impulsively on the cheek and left the study to go up to her room, but, while she showered and changed into a dress for dinner, she knew that she could never shut her mind to the reason for that dark cloud which cast such a terrible shadow over her future.

CHAPTER SIX

It was some weeks before Dale had the opportunity to give Joe Garrett that promised call to invite him and Tony over for the Friday evening.

'I can't say whether Tony will be free that evening, but I'll be there,' Joe Garrett told her. 'What time?'

'Seven-thirty?'

'That will be fine.'

'We look forward to seeing you, then,' said Dale, smiling as she lowered the receiver on to its cradle.

Joe Garrett's voice had sounded excited and almost boyish, and she could only hope that this meeting with Alex would live up to his expectations.

The rest of the week passed swiftly, and Dale was alone in the living-room on the Friday evening when the doorbell rang. A strange excitement surged through her when she got up to let Joe in, and she was pleasantly surprised to see that Tony had, after all, been able to accompany his father. He was dressed casually in beige slacks and matching jacket, and his blue shirt was open at the throat. Joe, however, was impeccably dressed, and most distinguished with his silvery-grey hair contrasting so heavily with his dark grey suit.

Dale crossed her fingers as she ushered them into the living-room, and she made the necessary introductions when Alex came down a few moments later. Tony shook hands almost carelessly, but Joe Garrett took Alex's hand firmly in his and bowed gallantly over it.

'Mrs Murray, it's a long-awaited pleasure to meet you,' he smiled directly into Alex's eyes and, for the

What made Marge burn the toast and miss her favorite soap opera?

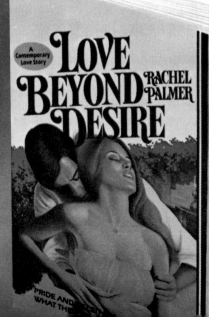

A Contemporary Love Story

LOVE BEYOND DESIRE

RACHEL PALMER

...At his touch, her body felt a familiar wild stirring, but she struggled to resist it. This is not love, she thought bitterly.

PRIDE AND
WHAT THE

A SUPERROMANCE™
the great new romantic novel she never wanted to end.
And it can be yours

FREE!

She never wanted it to end. And neither will you. From the moment you begin... *Love Beyond Desire,* your **FREE** introduction to the newest series of bestseller romance novels, **SUPERROMANCES.**

You'll be enthralled by this powerful love story... from the moment Robin meets the dark, handsome Carlos an<!-- -->finds herself involved in the jealousies, bitterness and secret passions of the Lopez family. Where her own forbidden love threatens to shatter her life.

Your FREE *Love Beyond Desire* is only the beginning. A subscription to **SUPERROMANCES** lets you look forward to a long love affair. Month after mont<!-- -->you'll receive four love stories of heroic dimension. Novels that will involve you in spellbinding intrigue, forbidden love and fiery passions.

You'll begin this series of sensuous, exciting contemporary novels... written by some of the top romance novelists of the day... with four each month.

And this big value... each novel, almost 400 pages of compelling reading... is yours for only $2.5C book. Hours of entertainment for so little. Far less tha a first-run movie or Pay-TV. Newly published novels, with beautifully illustrated covers, filled with page afte<!-- -->page of delicious escape into a world of romantic love... delivered right to your home.

A compelling love story of mystery and intrigue... conflicts and jealousies... and a forbidden love that threatens to shatter the lives of all involved with the aristocratic Lopez family.

┌─Mail this card today for your FREE gifts.

TAKE THIS BOOK
AND TOTE BAG FREE!

Mail to: **SUPERROMANCE**
2504 W. Southern Avenue, Tempe, Arizona 85282

YES, please send me FREE and without any obligation, my
SUPERROMANCE novel, *Love Beyond Desire.* If you do not hear
from me after I have examined my FREE book, please send me
the 4 new **SUPERROMANCE** books every month as soon as they
come off the press. I understand that I will be billed only $2.50 per
book (total $10.00). There are no shipping and handling or any
other hidden charges. There is no minimum number of books that
I have to purchase. In fact, I may cancel this arrangement at any
time. *Love Beyond Desire* and the tote bag are mine to keep as
FREE gifts even if I do not buy any additional books.

134-CIS-KAF6

Name	(Please Print)
Address	Apt. No.
City	
State	Zip
Signature	(If under 18, parent or guardian must sign.)

This offer is limited to one order per household and not valid to present
subscribers. We reserve the right to exercise discretion in granting membership.
If price changes are necessary you will be notified. Offer expires March 31, 1984.

PRINTED IN U.S.A.

SUPERROMANCE ™

EXTRA BONUS
MAIL YOUR ORDER
TODAY AND GET A
FREE TOTE BAG
FROM SUPERROMANCE.

Mail this card today for your FREE gifts.

SUPERROMANCE™
2504 W. Southern Avenue,
Tempe, Arizona 85282

Postage will be paid by addressee

First Class   Permit No. 70   Tempe, AZ

BUSINESS REPLY CARD

No Postage
Necessary
If Mailed
In The
United States

first time since knowing Alex, Dale saw her looking flustered.

'Won't you sit down?' Alex suggested, removing her fingers with obvious care from Joe's large hand.

The conversation seemed reluctant to flow. Joe was perhaps a little overawed, or perhaps Alex was simply aware of the extreme delicacy of the situation. Addressing one's admirers at a public function was one thing, Dale began to realise, but confronting one of them in one's own living-room was another.

Sheena made a timely entrance with a tray of coffee, and over a cup of aromatic brew the initial awkwardness diminished and everyone seemed to relax their guard. Joe succeeded finally in swinging the conversation round to Alex's books. This was a field in which Alex could become quite animated, and as Joe questioned her knowledgeably Alex emerged from her reserved shell.

'They seem to be getting on like a house on fire,' Tony murmured eventually when the discussion at the other end of the room had continued for a length of time.

'They do, don't they,' Dale admitted, glancing in Joe and Alex's direction.

Seeing them together like that made Dale realise what a striking couple they would make. They had the same interests, and they both enjoyed travelling, but . . .

'How long will you still be working for Mrs Murray?' Tony interrupted her wayward thoughts.

'A few months, perhaps. I'm not sure.'

'What will you do when you've finished your job here?'

'I haven't decided yet.'

A hint of anxiety invaded Tony's hazel eyes. 'I hope you're not going to leave Amanzimtoti?'

'I might.'

'Look,' he said earnestly. 'I could always find you a job somewhere.'

A humorous smile curved her mouth, and she placed her hand briefly over Tony's. 'That's sweet of you, but I'll manage on my own.'

They sat in silence for a moment, listening to Alex and Joe's discussion on the medicinal value of the bark of the flamboyant tree, then Tony drew Dale's attention away from them again.

'There's a dance at the hotel next week Saturday,' he said. 'Will you go with me?'

'I don't know, I——' She smiled ruefully. 'I can't dance.'

'Neither can I,' Tony grinned, 'but let's go and give it a bash?'

Dale considered this for a moment, wondering whether she ought not to refuse his invitation, then she changed her mind. 'I'd like to go with you.'

'Fine,' Tony said eagerly. 'I'll pick you up at seven, then?'

'Yes.'

Joe Garrett rose to his feet shortly after nine. 'We must not outstay our welcome, but perhaps we could meet again some day soon.'

'I'd like that,' said Alex at once, and a few minutes later Dale was standing beside Alex as they watched Joe's station wagon disappearing down the drive.

'What did you think of him?' Dale asked inquisitively when they entered the house and locked the front door behind them.

'Of Joe Garrett, you mean?' Alex smiled thoughtfully. 'He seemed a nice, interesting man.'

'And attractive, wouldn't you say?' Dale questioned mischievously, and Alex laughed selfconsciously.

'Attractive, yes, in a rugged sort of way,' she admitted.

'Tony has invited me to a dance at the hotel next Saturday,' Dale changed the subject.

'Will you be going?'

'Yes,' Dale laughed softly as they went upstairs. 'Neither of us can dance, so I can only hope we don't ruin each other's feet for life!'

Dale went shopping during the following week and bought a pale green lacy evening gown. She was going to her first dance, and she was more than a little nervous about it.

'Relax!' Alex ordered on that Saturday evening as she zipped her into her dress and turned her around so that she could inspect her appearance. 'You look lovely, and you're going to enjoy yourself.'

Dale clung to that thought, and it helped her over her initial bout of nerves when she arrived at the hotel with Tony. He knew most of the young people their own age and, instead of sitting alone as she had feared, they joined up with a few of his friends to form a party of eight. Tony was fun to be with, and she enjoyed herself, even though their dancing could not have been termed as anything other than a shuffle across the crowded floor.

Halfway through the evening the band lapsed into disco music, and everyone leapt excitedly to their feet, but Dale hesitated dubiously.

'There's nothing to it,' Tony laughed, pulling her to her feet. 'Follow me, and let the music take you where it wants to.'

That was easier said than done, Dale thought nervously, but with Tony to guide and encourage her, she soon forgot her nervousness, and relaxed with the beat of the music.

'We should do this again some time,' Tony said when he drove her home late that evening.

'It was fun,' she sighed happily. 'I never imagined dancing could be so enjoyable.'

The tanginess of the sea was in the air when he

walked her to the the door, but he had gone silent as if he were brooding about something, and she wondered whether she ought to question him about it.

'I have to go away for a few months to do my military training,' he confided in her eventually. 'Will you wait for me?'

Dale withdrew from him inwardly, but she took great care in the choice of her words. 'I shall pray for you, and I don't doubt that I shall still be here when you return.'

'That isn't what I meant,' he said impatiently.

'I know.' She lowered her gaze sadly. 'I would like to be your friend, Tony, but there can never be anything more between us.'

'Why not?' he demanded stubbornly, his hands gripping her shoulders lightly and his glance fixed on her pale face in the moonlight.

'Friendship is all I shall ever have to offer you.'

'Is there someone else?'

She shrugged off his hands and turned away to hide the pain in her eyes. 'At the moment I don't envisage a future for myself with any man, and please don't ask me to explain. I'm deeply touched that you should think of me in that way, but I don't want you to consider me as anything more than a friend.'

Tony was silent for what seemed like an eternity, and she was beginning to suspect that she had hurt him when he asked: 'If I write to you will you answer my letters?'

'Yes, of course,' she said, expelling the air slowly from her lungs. 'I shall write to you as often as I can.'

'I'll come and see you before I go,' he promised, turning her to face him and kissing her unexpectedly on the cheek, then he walked down the steps towards his car and drove away.

Dale lingered out on the scented terrace a while

longer. She felt disturbed and a little sad, but she finally shrugged off this feeling and went inside.

The living-room light had been left on, but, as her hand went out to the switch against the wall, a man rose from one of the wing-backed chairs to confront her, and the unexpectedness of finding someone there sent a cold blast of fear through her before she recognised the tall, lean man facing her.

'*Rick!*' she gasped, her hand at her throat as she sagged against the door jamb. 'You—you gave me a fright!'

His dark gaze slid over her, but instead of apologising, he said abruptly, 'Want some coffee?'

'Yes, please,' she breathed, her heart still beating with a mixture of fright and joy as she sat down in the chair facing the one he had vacated. 'When did you arrive?' she asked when he had poured coffee from a flask and handed her a cup.

'Just after eight this evening,' he said, resuming his seat and studying her so intently that she squirmed inwardly, then a germ of suspicion awakened within her.

'You haven't been waiting up for me, have you?'

'I wanted to make sure you got home safely.'

Dale was not quite certain whether she ought to feel flattered or annoyed, but she decided to let it pass as she studied him unobtrusively over the rim of her cup. In black corded pants and a black sweater he looked lean and powerful, and a weakness invaded her body that left her feeling intensely vulnerable. She loved him; she loved him so much that she ached for the freedom to nestle in his strong arms and bury her face against his solid chest, but her mind was drifting into a dangerous area, and she forced herself to remember that he could never feel anything but contempt for her.

'Did Melissa come with you?' she felt compelled to break the silence between them.

'Not this time.' His dark glance flicked over her slender, yet shapely figure in the pale green evening gown. 'You've grown up these past three months.'

'Have I?' she asked with a casualness she did not feel.

'In another four months from now you'll be twenty-one, and quite free to do as you please.'

'You've never restricted me in any way in the past, and I've always felt free to do as I please.'

'Except in one instance,' he corrected, his mouth twisting derisively. 'I gave you no choice about coming here to work for Alex.'

'That was for the best,' she said quietly, veiling her eyes to hide the turmoil raging in her mind and her soul. 'I enjoy working for Alex.'

Rick was silent for a moment, then he asked abruptly, 'Did you have a pleasant evening out with Tony Garrett?'

'Yes, I did,' she answered truthfully, placing her empty cup in the tray on the low table between them.

'Are you in love with him?' he shot the question at her, but his courtroom tactics did not shake her guard.

'I like his company.'

'That doesn't answer my question.'

'Being my guardian doesn't give you the right to pry into my personal feelings, Rick,' she argued quietly after pausing momentarily for thought, and his mouth tightened in a way which she could only interpret as anger.

'You'd better go up to bed,' he ordered tersely, getting to his feet and forcing her in this way to do the same. 'It's almost one o'clock.'

With her evening purse and wrap clutched in her hands she said goodnight, and walked out of the living-room. He did not follow her, but she felt his eyes burning into her back until she reached the hall.

Her breathing was rapid as she climbed the stairs up to her room, and for some inexplicable reason she was close to tears, but she choked them back and forced herself to remain calm. There was no future for her in loving Rick, she had to remember that, and adapt to it. She had to remember, too, that he belonged to Melissa, and Melissa was a much better proposition in every respect.

Dale went to bed, but she tossed about restlessly for almost an hour before she heard Rick's footsteps in the passage outside her door, and only when she heard him go into his room did she finally go to sleep.

Rick did not come down to breakfast the following morning, but Dale did not question Alex about him, and went instead for a walk on the beach where, even during the autumn and winter months, colourful umbrellas dotted the coastline, and bathers ventured into the warm Indian ocean.

She walked slowly along the promenade in front of the holiday flats until she reached the lagoon, then she took off her sandals and strolled back along the beach. The sea fascinated her. It heaved and subsided as if manipulated by a giant hand, and the waves rushed to the shore like magnificent white horses, only to disintegrate at her feet, then it drew back, tugging at the soft sand beneath her toes. There was music and majesty in the never-ending rhythm of the sea, and she respected it in all its many facets.

The sun was climbing higher in the cloudless sky as she turned away from the sea to return home, and her heart leapt into her throat when she approached the steps leading up to the promenade. Rick was there, leaning against the iron railings, and the perfect cut of his white summer suit accentuated the width of his shoulders and the lean, hard strength of his tall body.

'Your boy-friend didn't turn up this morning, I

see,' he remarked cynically when she reached his side, and she was instantly annoyed.

'If you so badly want to meet him, Rick, then I can arrange it.'

He smiled twistedly. 'I wonder what happened to that quiet little girl who at times could hardly open her mouth when she was spoken to.'

'I don't like the feeling that I'm being spied on,' she said coldly, seating herself on the nearest bench and brushing the sand off her feet before she slipped on her sandals.

'No one is spying on you, you little idiot,' he contradicted harshly, going down on his haunches in front of her and brushing the sand off her feet with his handkerchief, then he took her feet in his strong hands, slipped on her sandals, and secured the straps. 'I came down here to wait for you to save you an unnecessary walk up all those steps to the house.'

'You came to fetch me?' she asked incredulously, finding it an odd experience to have Rick kneeling at her feet.

'To take you for a drive down the coast with me, yes,' he nodded, straightening and taking her hands to pull her to her feet.

'Oh!'

'Oh!' he mocked her cruelly. 'Don't I get an apology for being unjustly accused of spying?'

Dale stared up into those unfathomable eyes and found the anger and irritation drain away from her to be replaced by remorse. 'I apologise.'

His expression did not soften, and his hand was hard on her arm as he said tersely, 'My car is up this way.'

Neither of them spoke until she was seated beside him in his white Mercedes, and she was forced to recall the one and only other occasion when she had

been driven somewhere by Rick. He had taken her from the Academy to his home, and on that day she had been overawed and nervous in his austere presence. Now she was simply nervous and bewildered by his unexpected invitation to go for a drive with him down the coast.

'Where are we going?' she asked, taking her eyes off the ribbon of road which sliced through the green and picturesque countryside.

'Anywhere and everywhere.' He glanced at her and smiled briefly. 'Does it matter?'

'You're in a strange mood this morning,' she told him, trying desperately to recover from that melting warmth aroused by his unexpected smile.

'What makes you think so?'

'You don't usually go anywhere or do anything without a specific purpose in mind,' she said almost accusingly.

'Who told you I don't have something specific in mind for this morning?' he demanded, and once again that faint suggestion of a smile hovered about his mouth.

'If you do, then may I know what it is?'

'I'll tell you later,' he said, and Dale knew better than to question him further.

It was a long, relaxing drive south past Port Shepstone and Margate, and she was beginning to think they were going as far as Port Edward when Rick turned in at Ramsgate with its blue lagoon and atmosphere of utter contentment. They stopped for something to drink at the Teahouse with its thatched roof, then they went a little farther to where cottages were being built among the wild strelitzias and palms. Rick parked his car, and when Dale walked with him towards one of the cottages it felt to her as if she were entering a small part of Eden situated in the serene semi-wilderness, but

civilisation, unbelievably, was just beyond the next sand dune.

'When I was here a month ago only the foundations had been laid. Now, as you can see, it's roof-high,' Rick enlightened her as they approached one of the more secluded cottages and, raising a questioning eyebrow at her, he asked, 'Shall we have a look around inside?'

She nodded mutely, and he took her arm to help her over the rubble the builders had left lying about when they had packed up for the weekend.

The smell of concrete mingled with the tangy smell of the sea as Rick took her through the cottage, pointing out the various rooms, and her imagination ran wild with all the possible ways to transform it into a comfortable hideout.

'This could be the ideal place for weekends and holidays,' he said as if he had read her thoughts. 'It's quiet and peaceful, and the beach is practically on one's doorstep for swimming, fishing, or whatever recreation one might prefer.'

'Are you having it built?' she questioned him for the first time.

'No, but I'm thinking of buying it.' He looked down at her from his great height and raised a quizzical eyebrow. 'Do you like it?'

'Well . . . yes, I . . . it ought to be very nice once it's completed,' she faltered, her throat tight and aching with misery. 'Has Melissa seen it?'

'Not yet.' He took her arm and gestured ahead. 'Mind that scaffolding.'

They walked out of the cottage, stepping over planks and steel pipes lying about, and those few seconds were all Dale needed to recover her composure.

'You have a natural garden here,' she could not prevent herself from saying enthusiastically. 'All you need is a patch of lawn.'

'That's what I thought,' Rick agreed. 'Shall we go for a walk along the beach?'

Dale nodded and took off her sandals once they reached the beach. To her surprise, Rick did the same. He took off his shoes and socks, and rolled his pants up to below his knees.

They strolled through the shallow water, not touching, and not speaking, and the perfect peace of that little haven was disturbed only by the sound of the surf and the mewing of the seagulls. Dale fell instantly in love with it all, but she still wondered why Rick had shown it to *her* instead of Melissa, who would, after all, be the one to live there with him when he had the opportunity to break away from his law practice.

It hurt to think of it, but she had to. There was no purpose in dwelling on futile hopes that Rick might ever care for her in any special way, and even if he did, there would always be that awful shadow between them.

'There's some excellent material along this part of the coast for an artist like yourself,' Rick finally broke the silence between them when they turned back the way they had come.

'So I've noticed,' she smiled a little sadly.

'Is that what you want to do when you've finished this job with Alex?' Rick asked, glancing down at her, but she avoided his probing eyes.

'I haven't quite decided yet.'

'You may feel quite free to use the cottage, if you wish.'

Surprised, she glanced up at him. 'You're going to buy it, then?'

'Yes,' he smiled, and her knees turned instantly to water.

'You would actually consider letting me stay here alone?' she asked in disbelief.

'I know Mother would love to come and stay here with you.' There was a hint of humour in his eyes. 'You know how she likes to have someone she can fuss over.'

But what about Melissa? she wondered. And what about the weekends and holidays he had contemplated spending there? It didn't quite make sense, but she let it pass for the moment.

'I'll consider your offer,' she said at length. 'Thank you.'

'Let's go and have lunch,' he suggested, his hand resting against the hollow of her back as they walked along the narrow path among the wild succulents to where he had parked his Mercedes. 'I know a place here that serves the most excellent crayfish.'

'But what about Alex?' she protested, conscious of the warmth of his hand through the thin cotton of her dress. 'Won't she be expecting us home for lunch?'

'I told her we'd eat out somewhere,' Rick put her mind at rest.

They brushed the sand off their feet with an old towel Rick had in the trunk of his car, and put on their shoes, but Dale felt a pang of regret when they drove away from the place she had dubbed secretly, 'Little Eden'.

They had lunch at a delightful little inn, and with the bottle of wine Rick had ordered it felt almost like a celebration to Dale. Perhaps they were celebrating his decision to buy the cottage, but Dale chose silently to celebrate the fact that this was the first time Rick had actually taken her out somewhere. It was foolish to pretend that it meant anything to him, but just for a little while she *did* pretend to herself that he had invited her out because he enjoyed her company, and had wanted to be with her as much as she wanted to be with him.

The dream did not last long, and when they arrived home later that afternoon Dale forced her thoughts back to reality. Rick had asked her to accompany him down to Ramsgate simply because he did not fancy going alone to inspect the progress they had made at the cottage, and for a time he had made her believe that her opinion was of importance to him. It was nice of him, even perhaps a little kind, but that was all.

After dinner that evening they sat out on the terrace where the air was permeated with the scent of the night flowers. The dark, velvety sky was studded with stars, and the full moon cast a silvery glow across Alex's beautiful garden.

'It's a lovely night for a walk on the beach,' Rick announced eventually. 'Do you two ladies perhaps want to join me?'

'I feel too abominably lazy,' Alex yawned, stretching in her cane chair.

'What about you, Dale?' he asked, getting to his feet and extending an inviting hand towards her.

Dale hesitated. 'If Alex doesn't mind staying home alone, then I'll go with you.'

'Of course I don't mind being left alone,' said Alex at once. 'Run along and enjoy yourself, my dear.'

Dale placed her hand in Rick's and allowed him to pull her to her feet, but he did not release her hand afterwards, and pulled it through his arm as they walked down the steps and took the path towards the side gate which Dale used so often when she went down to the beach.

They walked in silence; a companionable silence that needed no conversation to mar this beautiful evening. The breeze on the beach was cool and fresh and, with her arm still linked through Rick's, they walked in the direction of the lagoon. His nearness was close to a pleasant ache, but she did not want to think

dark thoughts on such a beautiful night in the company of the man she would always love above all others.

'It's been a very relaxing day, and I've enjoyed your company very much,' Rick's deep, pleasant voice came close to echoing her own thoughts when they finally retraced their steps.

'I've enjoyed being with you,' she confessed unashamedly.

'Have you?'

'You're seldom this relaxed,' she told him, glancing up into his shadowed face. 'When you wear your stern, forbidding mask you're usually quite unapproachable, and you make me nervous.'

'And I didn't make you feel nervous today?' he questioned mockingly.

'No,' she laughed softly. 'You've been so very human for a change.'

'Have I now?' he drawled, and Dale bit her lip as she averted her glance.

'I suppose I shouldn't have said that.'

'I'm not objecting.' His free hand covered hers where it lay on his arm, and the pressure of his fingers sent a pleasurable warmth flowing up the length of her arm. 'It's simply that I have always considered myself extremely human, and now I hear something quite to the contrary,' he continued to mock her.

'We don't always see ourselves as others see us,' she replied softly, and was surprised to hear the soft rumble of laughter deep down in his throat.

'Perhaps not,' he agreed, and they continued their walk in silence until they opened the wooden gate and stepped into Alex's garden.

The scent of the night flowers was all around them as they walked beneath the natural arch formed by the trees, and she knew that she would always associate

the scent of these flowers with this wonderful day she
had spent with Rick.

'You remind me of the moonflower,' he spoke
suddenly beside her, forcing her to pause and turn to
face him. 'The moonflower hides its fragile bloom and
elusive fragrance under the blanket of night, and in the
daylight one will search in vain for it.'

There was all at once something electrifying in the
air between them, and her mind warned her to be on
her guard. 'Rick, I think . . .'

'You're a moonflower,' he interrupted her as if she
had not spoken. 'Fragile, fragrant, and so very lovely
this evening.'

His eyes glittered strangely in the moonlit darkness,
and she withdrew her hand from his arm, afraid
suddenly of what was happening between them. 'I
think we'd better go inside.'

Dale turned from him and, in her haste, she
tripped over the protruding root of a tree, but she
never collided with the moss-covered earth. His
arms cushioned her fall, and she clutched at him
instinctively to save herself, but her action threw
him off balance and almost brought him down on
top of her. Shocked and breathless, she could do
nothing but stare helplessly up into his dark,
shadowy face above hers as he kneeled beside her
and cradled her against him. The heat of his body
invaded her own, and her heart was beating
uncontrollably fast when he lowered his head and
took possession of her parted lips.

It had all happened much too fast, and the barriers
she had taken such care to erect came crashing down
as she felt the swift, heavy beat of his heart against her
own. There was no gentleness in his kiss, only a harsh,
sensual demand, and she responded to it a little
wildly, but only for a moment. His contempt that
night of the storm had cut too deep, and then there

was Melissa Arnell, whom Dale dared not overlook. There had been a certain magic about walking on the moonlit beach with Rick, and perhaps some of that magic had touched him too, but whatever it was that had prompted him to react in this manner, she dared not let him continue for fear that he might guess the feelings that lay locked up in her heart.

Dale stirred in the circle of his arms, her hands on his wide shoulders pushing instead of clutching, and he raised his head at once to draw her up on to her feet with him, but he did not release her entirely. He was breathing a little heavily, and so was she as she leaned back in his arms. That magical something was still there between them, but she knew she had to do something about it when his dark head dipped once more towards hers, and she had to do something quickly.

'Let me go, Rick,' she heard herself say in a voice that sounded amazingly calm and quiet in comparison with her clamouring emotions at that moment, and he released her at once, stepping back into the shadows so that his expression was hidden from her, but she felt certain that a glimmer of contempt was lurking in his dark eyes once again.

'You'd better go into the house,' he said tersely, and there was a hint of hateful mockery in his voice when he added: 'Take care this time that you don't trip and fall, because I shan't be there to pick you up.'

Dale blessed the darkness as she felt her face become heated with embarrassment and, not waiting to hear more, she fled from him across the garden and into the house.

She spent a restless night wondering in what kind of mood she would find Rick the following morning, but he had already left for Durban when she went down to breakfast. She felt relieved and disappointed at the

same time, and this feeling remained with her throughout the rest of the day.

Her mind ceaselessly and cruelly conjured up the way Rick had held her and kissed her. Surely it had meant *something* to him? Or had he perhaps thought that she had tripped purposely to manipulate herself into his arms in order to invite his kisses? Oh, no, *no!* The latter was unthinkable! Rick was not stupid, he would know when something was planned and when it was not, and she could only hope that he would know how very much she had wanted to avoid the very thing that had happened. A dreadful coldness invaded her heart as one other thought entered her mind. He could simply have seen fit to amuse himself with the illegitimate daughter of a demented woman! It was possible, but when she gave the matter more sensible thought, she could not believe that Rick fitted into this category.

'You've been in a rather distracted mood today,' Alex remarked teasingly when they pushed their work aside shortly after five that afternoon. 'Don't tell me you're missing Rick?'

'I am, in a way,' Dale admitted, blushing scarlet, and Alex observed her speculatively.

'You're fond of Rick, aren't you.'

It was a statement, not a query, and Dale lowered her gaze to her clenched hands in her lap to hide her misery. 'Yes, I'm fond of him.'

A tense silence followed, then Alex got up and seated herself on the corner of Dale's desk. 'Don't fall in love with that stone-hearted brother of mine, Dale. You'll only get hurt, and I wouldn't want that to happen . . . not for anything in the world.'

'It's too late, I love him already,' her heart cried, but aloud she said: 'Do you think he's going to marry Melissa?'

'Who knows?' Alex shrugged. 'She's lasted longer

than anyone else, and even though I don't like her, I have to admit they're well suited to each other.'

Dale gazed up at her curiously. 'What do you mean?'

'They're both equally hard and cold,' Alex laughed harshly, getting to her feet and wandering across to the window where she stood for a moment with her back turned towards Dale, then she swung round sharply. 'Don't misunderstand me, my dear. I love Rick with all his faults, because I know what has made him this way.'

They faced each other across the room in silence, and something in Alex's dark eyes made Dale realise that she had quite accidentally been told something which no one, perhaps, was supposed to know about.

'You can't stop now, Alex,' she said quietly, her body rigid as a statue. 'What is it that's made Rick the way he is today?'

'If he finds out that I——'

'He won't ever hear it from me,' Dale assured her in that same quiet voice, and Alex relented with a sad little sigh.

'There was a girl once. They were both twenty-four, and they were both studying law. He was crazy about her, and they were going to be married. On the night of their engagement party she didn't turn up, and Rick went to look for her. His search for her ended in a hospital where she'd been admitted after being involved in an accident, and she died minutes after his arrival.' Alex stared out of the window and sighed heavily. 'I think something died in Rick that night too.'

A great sadness welled up inside Dale, and with it came a certain understanding of the man she had learned to love, but that love would never be returned. He might marry someone like Melissa, but love would

never enter into it for him, and Dale wept in her heart for him, as well as herself.

She crossed the room to where Alex stood, and touched her arm lightly. 'Thank you for telling me.'

Alex nodded absently, and Dale left her there alone in the study to go up to her room. Her compassionate heart ached for Rick, but he would never know, and neither would he care.

CHAPTER SEVEN

The telephone on Alex's desk rang the following morning, but Dale paid little attention to what was being said while she grappled mentally with Alex's disorderly notes. The book was almost half way to completion, and if they continued at this pace it would be ready to send to the publishers before the end of that year.

'That was Joe Garrett,' said Alex when she replaced the receiver and had gained Dale's attention. 'He's invited me out to dinner this evening.'

Dale was delighted at the news, but Alex's frowning uncertainty made her ask quickly, 'I hope you accepted?'

'I did ... that is ... on condition that you don't mind eating alone this evening.'

'Of course I don't mind,' Dale assured her promptly. 'I would have hated to think you refused him because of me.'

A thread of excitement seemed to wind itself through the day, and Dale wondered at times whether Alex felt it too, but Alex was very much like her brother. They were both equally adept at masking their feelings, and this was something for which Dale envied them.

Dale was relaxing in her room that evening when there was a knock on her door, and when Alex walked in Dale set aside the magazine she had been paging through to stare at the tall, slender woman with the striking features.

'You look absolutely stunning,' said Dale, her appreciative glance taking in the wine-red evening

gown which clung softly to Alex's still remarkably youthful figure.

'Would you believe I'm nervous?' Alex smiled faintly, seating herself on the bed beside Dale and fiddling with the clasp of her evening bag.

'Why on earth should you be nervous?' Dale asked in surprise.

'I haven't been out with a man in . . .' She paused briefly for thought, then laughed selfconsciously as she concluded, 'Oh, *years!*'

Dale studied her gravely, and for the first time since knowing Alex, she asked: 'Why did you never marry again?'

'At first I wasn't interested,' Alex replied, getting to her feet and moving about restlessly. 'My brief marriage to Nigel Murray had been enough to turn me off men for quite some time, and later I became too busy to be bothered with a husband cluttering up my life.' She smiled derisively as she paused in front of Dale. 'There's one other reason why I decided eventually that marriage was not for me, and it's a very important reason. Very few men would be satisfied with a wife who traipses all over the country periodically in search of material for her books. It would result in arguments and tantrums, and I couldn't work under that sort of pressure.'

'What you need is a man who shares your interests, and who not only enjoys travelling about but has the time for it,' Dale announced, her mind very busy selecting the right man for Alex.

'Where does one find a man like that?' Alex questioned mockingly, at the precise moment that Dale's sensitive ears picked up the sound of an approaching vehicle.

'There's one coming up your drive right this very minute.'

'So there is,' Alex laughed softly, then she leaned

over hurriedly and kissed Dale on the cheek. 'Don't wait up for me.'

Her subtle perfume still lingered in the room after she had gone, and some minutes later Dale went downstairs to sit down to a solitary meal. She did not mind being alone, but she was scarcely aware of what she was eating. Her thoughts were occupied with Alex and Joe Garrett, and she found herself hoping something would come of their relationship. They were ideal for each other, but there was always the physical angle to consider. If that spark was missing between them, then nothing on earth could put it there.

Dale's mind wandered in Rick's direction, but she pulled herself up sharply. There was no future for her with Rick, or with any other man, she decided eventually when she returned to her room. Her past was too damning, and there could never be a happy ending for her even if Rick did begin to see her as something other than his ward. He had kissed her twice, but circumstances had led to it, and she was certain that most men might have reacted in the same way. Perhaps someone who had been unaware of her heritage might not have looked upon her with such contempt, but that, she supposed, was the only difference. She had to remember who she was, and where she came from, and she would have to be more careful in future. She planned concentrating on her sketching when Alex's book was completed, and she wanted to experiment a great deal more in oils, as well as watercolours. It was something to look forward to, having a place of her own where she could work, and it was something which would absorb her totally.

Rick's cottage at Ramsgate came to mind, but she could not accept his offer. *Little Eden.* A smile plucked at her mouth as she sat down at her desk beside the window and, opening her sketch pad, began to sketch

each room in the cottage as she imagined it ought to look when it was completed and furnished. The breeze that stirred the curtains was scented, and it filled her room until the subtle fragrance of the night flowers was all around her while she sketched. Her pencil moved rapidly to match her enthusiasm, and with the help of coloured pencils she created the décor she had envisaged. It was senseless to dream when Melissa would be the one to choose the décor, Dale told herself, but without dreams one might as well be dead.

The telephone rang shortly after ten, and Dale took the call on the extension in Alex's bedroom.

'I hope I didn't get you out of bed?' Tony's voice came clearly across the line.

'No, I was sketching,' she replied and, recalling their last conversation, she asked: 'I suppose you'll be leaving soon?'

'I was called up sooner than I expected,' he replied. 'I'm leaving very early tomorrow morning.'

Dale did not attempt to hide her disappointment. 'I was hoping I would have the opportunity to see you again.'

'I've been rather busy, but I'll write to you.'

'I shall look forward to your letters, and take care of yourself.'

'By the way,' Tony changed the subject quickly, 'I think my father has fallen for Mrs Murray in a big way.'

Dale crossed her fingers mentally. 'Do you think so?'

'Positive,' Tony stated firmly.

'But this evening is only the second time they're seeing each other,' Dale tried to reason sensibly.

'I know,' Tony laughed, 'but the signs are all there.'

'What signs?'

'He's never looked at another woman since my mother died, and it's really something for my father to

get toffed up to take a woman out to dinner,' he told her with a hint of humour in his voice.

She absently fingered the silk scarf lying on Alex's bed. 'Would you mind very much if something came of it?'

'I think it would be fun having a famous authoress as a stepmother,' Tony laughed loudly, but he sobered almost at once. 'Seriously, though, my father has been pretty lonely, and it's time he thought of his own happiness for a change.'

They said goodbye a few moments later, and Dale wandered back to her own room in a thoughtful mood. It was perhaps silly to speculate, but if Joe Garrett was almost halfway to falling in love with Alex, then all that remained was to find out how Alex felt about him, and that was exactly what Dale intended to do.

She finished off her sketches during the next hour, but she was no longer concentrating on what she was doing. Her conversation with Tony continued to swivel through her mind, and she found herself listening intently for the sound of a car while she bathed and prepared herself to go to bed. She had no intention of waiting up for Alex, but she was still awake when she heard her come in and, despite the late hour, she left her room and knocked on Alex's bedroom door.

'May I come in?' asked Dale, opening the door before Alex could reply to her knock.

'I thought you'd be in bed and asleep ages ago,' Alex remarked, casting a surprised glance in Dale's direction.

'I was in bed, but I wasn't asleep,' Dale explained, observing Alex closely as she took off her necklace and kicked off her shoes. 'How was your evening?'

'It was interesting.'

Dale studied her attractive features intently. 'Is that all it was? Interesting?'

'No,' Alex laughed suddenly, stepping out of her dress and draping it across a hanger. 'It's a long time since someone has succeeded in making me feel fragile and feminine, and it's something I thought I'd never experience again.'

'Joe made you feel like that?' Dale questioned her with a calmness that belied the excitement churning through her.

'Some men have the ability to make a woman feel special, and Joe Garrett is certainly one of them,' said Alex, and her dark eyes were unmistakably dreamy when she sat down on the bed in her slip and wrapped her arms about herself as if she were hugging her thoughts to her breast.

'I'm glad you enjoyed yourself,' Dale murmured, feeling suddenly like an intruder as she edged her way towards the door. 'Goodnight, Alex.'

Dale felt again that stirring of excitement and hope when she was alone in her room, but as she switched off the light she could only pray that these two lonely people would find each other somehow. It was safer to think of someone else rather than herself, but she could not deny the longing that came close to an ache deep down inside her.

Dale was sitting out on the terrace late one afternoon when a young man came walking up the drive, and he glanced at Dale with some uncertainty as he sprinted up the steps towards her.

'Miss Palmer?' he queried, and she rose slowly to her feet.

'That's right.'

A small package, wrapped neatly in brown paper, was thrust into her hands. 'I was asked to deliver this to you.'

'Thank you,' Dale murmured, feeling a little bewildered as she fingered the package, but before she

could ask the young man who had sent it, he had leapt down the steps and was walking hurriedly down the drive towards the exit.

The paper crackled between her exploratory fingers. It was a square object, but she could not determine what it might be, and she was oddly hesitant to open it. Impatient with herself, she finally tugged at the string holding the wrapping together, and when it fell away she folded open the paper to find a pressed flower behind glass in a small square frame. It was a moonflower, but a slightly different species from the one growing at the bottom end of Alex's garden, and she knew then that there was only one person on this earth who could have sent it to her. *Rick!*

Her knees felt ridiculously weak, and she sat down heavily in the chair she had vacated only minutes earlier. She clutched the small frame in her lap with hands that were trembling, and the feelings that were racing through her at that moment were much too muddled to analyse. Had Rick sent her the pressed moonflower to mock her once again, or had he meant it that night when he had compared her to this fragrant night blossom? Dale shook her head confusedly. She could understand and accept his mockery, but the latter was too impossible to even think about. It bordered too close on something she never could and never *would* accept from Rick. But what other reason could there be for this unexpected gift to remind her of that evening he had kissed her so passionately in the scented garden?

Thrusting the small frame as well as the wrapping into the pockets of her wide skirt, she went up to her room before Alex found her out there on the terrace and asked awkward questions.

She sat on her bed and stared at the delicate, oval-shaped petals from which the moisture had been pressed with such care to preserve the flower, if not

the fragrance, and she wished she knew the reason behind this unusual gift. It was hopeless trying to fathom Rick's motives, and she finally relinquished the effort. She ought to telephone him and thank him for the gift. That was the accepted procedure, but she shied away from the thought, and finally decided against it.

A few weeks later, when Rick brought his mother and Melissa down to Amanzimtoti with him for the weekend, Dale could still not bring herself to mention his gift, and for that reason she avoided him as much as she avoided being alone with the cold-eyed Melissa.

Dale was awake long before breakfast on the Sunday morning, and the air was so cool and fresh outside that she decided to go for a walk on the beach before everyone else was awake. There was not a cloud in the sky, and the early morning sun touched the dew-wet earth gently, making it glitter and sparkle at her feet.

The beach was still deserted, and the tangy sea air was in her mouth and her nostrils as she started off across the sand. The restless ocean swelled, sending frothy waves crashing to the shore. It filled her ears, deafening the sound of the man who had called her name as he followed her slim, straight figure along the beach, and she was made aware of him only when a heavy hand on her shoulder swung her round to face him with a startled look in her eyes.

'You've been avoiding me for some reason,' Rick accused bluntly, his fingers biting into her shoulder. 'And don't deny it!'

'I wasn't going to,' she said, her veiled glance sliding over his wide shoulders and slim hips in black slacks and sweater, and her pulse quickened when his grip on her shoulder relaxed to become a caress instead of a punishment.

'I think you owe me an explanation.'

It was a command, not a request, and she knew

better than to evade the issue. 'Why did you send me that moonflower?' she heard herself ask with a frankness that surprised even herself. 'Was it to mock me?'

His mouth tightened, and his hand fell away from her shoulder. 'Is that what you thought?'

She lowered her gaze uncomfortably, and a bright veil of silky hair fell forward to hide her embarrassment. 'I haven't known what to think, and that's why I'm asking.'

'I saw it quite by chance in the window of a curio shop near my office, and it made me think of you, so I sent it along to you with the first person who happened to be passing this way.' His strong hands framed her face and raised it to his. 'There was nothing nasty or sinister attached to that gift. It was simply a reminder to me of a wonderful day spent together, and I hoped you would see it that way too.'

Dale stared a long way up into his dark, probing eyes, and she felt her insides tremble with a longing that would not be stilled. 'I owe you an apology, Rick.'

'I think you do,' he smiled faintly.

'Will you forgive me, and let me thank you properly?'

'When you look at me like that with your big blue eyes I find I can forgive you anything,' he teased lightly and, raising her own hands until her fingers were locked in the crisp dark hair at the nape of his neck, she drew his head down to hers, and kissed him briefly on the lips.

'Thank you, Rick,' she whispered, letting her hands fall to her sides, and instantly overcome with shyness when she realised that it was the first time she had kissed him like that of her own volition.

His thumbs caressed her cheekbones, and she felt something melt inside her. His touch was no longer casual, it was deliberately sensual, and she sensed the

danger in prolonging this moment when she looked up into his dark eyes, but he seemed to become aware of her withdrawal before there was any need for her to say anything, and he released her almost abruptly.

'We're going to be late for breakfast,' he said as he turned away from her, and his voice was so cold and distant that it hurt.

They walked back to the house like strangers with nothing to say to each other, and for one awful moment she was horrifyingly close to tears, but somehow she managed to hold them back.

Melissa was out on the terrace when they arrived, and her beautiful features were tight with suppressed fury. 'Where on earth have you been?'

'Dale and I went for a walk on the beach,' Rick answered smoothly. 'If you'd been awake you could have joined us, Melissa.'

'If you'd taken the trouble to let me know you'd planned such an excursion then I might have joined you. Or was a morning stroll on the beach part of your duty as a guardian?' The silence was electrifying as Melissa smiled sweetly but venomously when she directed her cold grey glance at Dale. 'He really takes his responsibilities much too seriously, doesn't he, my dear?'

'He certainly does,' Dale replied stiffly without glancing at Rick, and she knew that if she did not get away at that moment she would burst into tears. 'If you'll excuse me, then I think I'll go up and see if Mrs Crawford is ready to come down to breakfast.'

Dale escaped into the house, and she somehow managed to look outwardly calm as she went up the carpeted stairs, but inwardly she was fuming like a volcano. Melissa had very cleverly reduced that early morning walk on the beach with Rick from something pleasant, to a dutiful, distasteful encounter. *No*, she decided charitably, she could not blame Melissa

entirely for the way she felt. Rick's cold and distant manner had a lot to do with the way she felt now, and frustration and despair finally succeeded in bringing those unwanted tears to her eyes which she had to dash away hastily before she knocked on Brenda Crawford's bedroom door and entered.

'Melissa was here looking for Rick not ten minutes ago,' Mrs Crawford exclaimed irritably, turning from the dressing-table mirror to face Dale. 'Really, that woman behaves as if she owns him, and I'm surprised he allows it!'

Dale thought it wiser not to respond to that remark. 'Are you ready to go down to breakfast?'

'Yes, my dear,' Brenda smiled as if she sensed Dale's reluctance to discuss Melissa Arnell, but when they reached the door she paused and turned towards Dale. 'Do you know, you're lovelier every time I see you?'

'It's kind of you to say so, Mrs Crawford,' Dale shied away from the unexpected compliment, but the older woman knew her too well to leave the matter there.

'I'm not simply flattering you, Dale,' she said gravely. 'It's the truth.'

Dale stared into those dark eyes and saw only that familiar warmth and sincerity, and she leaned forward impulsively to kiss Brenda on her soft cheek. 'Thank you, Mrs Crawford.'

'Before we go downstairs there's something I must ask you,' Brenda changed the subject. 'Has Rick perhaps mentioned something to you which might give me the idea as to what's the matter with him lately?'

'Rick never speaks to me about himself, or about his work,' Dale answered truthfully, and she could not quite veil the concern in her eyes. 'Is there something the matter?'

'He's so moody and so terribly morose lately, and it's been getting steadily worse ever since you came here to live with Alex.' Her dark eyes probed Dale's. 'You have no idea what it can be?'

If Melissa had been asked this question she would have said at once that the responsibility of having a ward was weighing too heavily on Rick's shoulders, but Dale was not too sure that she would have agreed with Melissa. Rick was not the sort of man to crack under pressure, and if he was troubled about something, then it most certainly had nothing to do with her being his ward.

'I have no idea at all, I'm afraid,' Dale said at length.

'I do hope he's not ill,' Brenda muttered anxiously.

'Perhaps he's been rather busy at the office lately.'

'That may be so,' Brenda nodded, then she gestured exasperatedly with her slender hands. 'Oh, if only he'd talk to me instead of leaving me to suspect the worst!'

'If it was something serious, then I'm sure he'd tell you about it.'

'I'm constantly telling myself that, but it doesn't always help,' the older woman smiled wanly, then she brushed aside the matter with a wave of her hand. 'Come on, we'd better not keep everyone waiting.'

The morning passed pleasantly enough for Dale while she stayed out of Melissa's way, and she was not exactly surprised when Joe Garrett arrived at Alex's invitation to join them for lunch that Sunday.

'I'm here to meet the family,' Joe winked at Dale when she let him in and took him through to the living-room, and she smiled inwardly at the thought of what must be going on behind his calm exterior.

'Joe!' Alex put down her glass of wine and came forward at once to take both his hands in hers. 'I'm so glad you could make it,' she smiled up at him with eyes that seemed unusually bright.

Dale moved away from what appeared to be a very private meeting despite the fact that three pairs of eyes were observing Alex and Joe intently from across the room, but before she had moved too far she heard Joe murmur something to Alex which sounded like, 'The sooner I meet them, the better.'

Did that mean what she thought it meant? Dale wondered. She was lost in thought for a moment while Alex introduced Joe Garrett to Mrs Crawford and Rick, but she did not miss the provocative flutter of Melissa's eyelashes as she extended her perfectly manicured hand towards Joe. Dale was instantly annoyed. Was Rick not enough for Melissa? Did she have to make an attempt to capture the attention of every man she met?

What happened next was something for which Melissa would most probably never forgive Joe. He clasped her hand briefly, then he turned away from her ravishing beauty and, without being impolite, he more or less ignored her existence for the rest of the afternoon. It had not been deliberate, but it had been decisive, and the obvious action of a man whose interests lay elsewhere. With Alex, perhaps?

Brenda Crawford took an instant liking to Joe, Dale could see that, and after lunch, when everyone lounged on the cool terrace, Dale saw Alex exchange glances with Rick, and he actually nodded as if he gave his approval.

Joe left early that afternoon, and Alex later went upstairs with Mrs Crawford to help her pack. Rick and Melissa wandered off somewhere and, with nothing better to do, Dale went up to her room to fetch her sketchpad. Seated in a secluded corner of the terrace, she made a few sketches simply for her own amusement, and when Rick returned to the terrace, alone, some minutes later, she noticed that he was in one of his scowling moods. She recalled her

conversation with Brenda that morning, and it left her wondering. Was there something seriously wrong?

Without so much as a glance in her direction, Rick lowered himself on to the cane recliner with its bright floral cushions, and arranged his lean length comfortably. He looked outwardly relaxed with his one knee raised, and an arm flung above his dark head, but Dale had an odd feeling that he was as tense as a tightly coiled spring. She flicked over a page in her book and, without actually intending to, she found herself sketching Rick. Her pencil moved swiftly across the paper, capturing him in the minutest detail, and every stroke was done with loving care, but she had not completed it to her satisfaction when he sat up half an hour later, and swung his feet down on to the stone-tiled floor.

'What are you sketching?' he asked, getting up and strolling towards her with his thumbs hooked into the narrow belt about his lean waist.

'Oh, nothing,' she replied evasively, her heart pounding uncomfortably as she snapped shut her sketchpad, and tried not to look like a child caught in the act of doing something it was not supposed to.

He held out an imperious hand. 'Let me see.'

'No, I——' The sketchpad was snatched from her hands before she had time to guess his intentions, and he was paging through it rapidly before she could prevent it. 'Rick, please give that back to me.'

'Is it something you don't want me to see, for some reason?' he smiled briefly, pausing to look down into her wide, troubled eyes, and she held out an imploring hand for the sketchpad he was paging through.

'Please, Rick.'

'You've made me much too curious,' he said, flicking over the remaining pages.

'No!' she cried anxiously, but it was too late. He had found what he had been looking for, and she wished the earth would open up beneath her as she watched his stern, expressionless features while he studied the sketch she had made of him.

'Was I smiling?' he asked at length.

'No,' she admitted truthfully, her voice no more than a croak. 'But I like you better when you do.'

That seemed to amuse him, for there was laughter in the eyes that met hers. 'May I have this?'

'I haven't finished it off properly,' she protested, nervous and embarrassed at the same time.

'It looks good enough to me,' he insisted, ripping it out and dropping her sketchpad into her lap. 'I'll keep it as a reminder to smile more often.'

She slanted a wary glance up at him as he folded the sheet of paper and slipped it into his shirt pocket. 'You're not angry?'

'Did you think I would be?'

'I wasn't sure.'

There was something in his eyes suddenly that made the breath still in her throat as he went down on to his haunches in front of her.

'Dale . . .'

She never knew what he was going to say, because Melissa stepped out on to the terrace at that precise moment.

'So there you are,' her clear, musical voice rang out. 'Isn't it about time we were leaving?'

Dale felt decidedly uncomfortable, but Rick appeared to be unperturbed as he rose to his feet and turned to face Melissa. 'We'll leave as soon as Mother is ready.'

The atmosphere was decidedly chilly after that. Dale did not like the icy venom in Melissa's eyes whenever she happened to glance in her direction, and she was thankful when they all left some minutes later.

'I love having the family for the weekend, but I just adore the peace and quiet when they're gone,' Alex sighed, almost echoing Dale's thoughts as they stood out on the terrace and watched Rick's Mercedes disappear down the drive.

Dale had a strong desire to laugh, but the tears were much too close, so she gave in to neither as she followed Alex into the silent house.

The weeks flowed into months during which Rick and Mrs Crawford came through for the occasional weekend, but Melissa never accompanied them again, for some reason. Dale often wondered about this, but she was not in a position to question Rick. They were seldom alone during his visits to Alex, Dale made certain of that, and his brooding manner disturbed her to the point where she believed she had not known him at all.

Joe Garrett also became a frequent visitor during these months, and Dale was beginning to suspect that their relationship had developed into something much more than friendship. They were always very discreet, but Dale's suspicions were confirmed when she walked into the living-room one evening to find them in a close embrace.

Alex blushed like a young girl as she tried to escape from Joe's embrace, but he kept a firm arm about her waist, and there was more than a humorous twinkle in his eyes when he turned towards Dale.

'You instigated our meeting, so we would like you to be the first to hear our news,' he said, his deep, gravelly voice more pronounced. 'Alex has agreed to become my wife.'

'Oh, I'm so happy for you both!' Dale exclaimed happily, rushing forward to kiss them both spontaneously. 'When is the great day to be?'

'I'd like to arrange it for this coming Saturday, but

Alex insists we should wait until after your twenty-first birthday.'

'Oh, no!' Dale replied hastily, sensing a hint of impatience in his voice. 'You don't have to do that.'

'Rick and Mother will be coming down that evening for your birthday, and by that time Tony will also be home again,' Alex explained calmly, then a look of pleading entered her eyes as she glanced up at Joe. 'I would like us to have his blessings before we think of setting a date.'

'It makes sense, I suppose,' Joe agreed ruefully, and Alex suddenly laughed up at him.

'You're just impatient, that's all,' she accused teasingly and, drawing his head down to hers, she kissed him on his rugged cheek.

'I'm sure you must still have a lot to discuss,' Dale intervened hastily, beginning to feel like an intruder on their privacy. 'I'll say goodnight and go up to bed.'

They were so absorbed in each other that Dale wondered afterwards whether they had heard her, but it did not matter. She was so happy for them, and she could only pray that nothing would happen to mar their future together.

A little stab of sadness shot through her at the realisation that she would never know that kind of happiness, but she thrust aside the thought almost at once for fear of becoming a victim of self-pity. She had so much in life to be thankful for and, if she chose to accept the offer she had received from Newton Gould to do illustrations for his company, she had a future to look forward to. What more could anyone want? Dale knew the answer to that only too well, but she was determined not to dwell on it. A home, a husband, and children! That was something she dared not wish for. She could make a home for herself, but having a husband and children was something she dared not contemplate.

During the next two weeks Dale had little time to think about herself. Alex's book was nearing completion and, much against Dale's wishes, Alex was making elaborate preparations for Dale's coming-of-age party on the Friday evening. Dale went flat-hunting in earnest, using every available spare moment to find what she wanted, and she was at last fortunate enough to find a flat on the beachfront with a splendid view of the sea. Alex was not too happy about this arrangement, but she had to agree in the end that Dale might be happier on her own. Rick was the final hurdle to be overcome. He would no doubt object violently to her decision, but once she was twenty-one she could do as she pleased, and he could not brush aside that fact.

Dale awoke early on her birthday. Alex had insisted that she sleep late, but habit dies hard, and she got up out of bed to draw the curtains aside. It was going to be a warm, spring day, she realised as she leaned out of the window to breathe the fresh, scented air deep into her lungs, and a smile hovered about her mouth despite that hint of sadness that stirred within her. She had arrived at the end of one era in her life, but she was on the brink of another, and as she watched the starlings building their nests in the trees she wondered what the future had in store for her.

There had been so much pain and disillusionment in the past that she wished she could forget it, but the past was the basis of her future, and on that crumbling foundation she would have to build her very existence.

CHAPTER EIGHT

At Dale's request the party that evening was a quiet affair with only Rick, Mrs Crawford, Joe and Tony present, and Alex was naturally there to act as hostess. Dale had stipulated most emphatically that there were to be no gifts, and that it would be enough simply to have everyone there to share in the occasion of her coming of age, but directly after Rick had poured champagne and proposed an elaborate toast, a large, brightly wrapped box was carried into the living-room.

'I know you said that you didn't want any presents,' Alex explained, 'but we all got together and decided to give you something we know you're going to need in future.'

Dale felt tears pricking her eyelids, but she blinked them away rapidly and put down her glass to open the parcel which had been placed on the floor at her feet. The wrapping came away with ease, but the cardboard box was so well sealed that it proved a little difficult.

Rick dipped his hand into his pocket and stepped forward, but Tony was there before him to lend a hand.

'Let me help you,' he said, flicking open his penknife as he knelt beside her on the carpet, and Dale glanced up briefly for some reason, to glimpse a strange tightening about Rick's mouth while Tony slit the seals.

Was Rick annoyed about something? she wondered vaguely, but, when Tony rose to his feet, she opened the flaps of the box, and promptly forgot about Rick's odd behaviour when she found herself staring at an array of equipment which would want to make any

artist rush into the nearest studio to try them out. There was an easel which could be adapted for large or small paintings, as well as oil paints and watercolours, with brushes of all sizes and description. Wrapped in tissue paper was a palette on which to mix paint, and a palette-knife, and right at the bottom of the box there was a roll of canvas with a supply of sketchbooks and pencils.

Dale was so overwhelmed that she was speechless. She was aware of an expectant silence in the room, as if everyone were waiting for her to say something, but she could not, and it was Rick, surprisingly, who sensed her predicament.

'You don't have to say anything,' he announced calmly, drawing her to her feet and placing a strong, steadying arm about her waist. 'We only have to look at your face to know you're wishing we would all go home so that you can try out that equipment.'

Amid the laughter Dale at last found her tongue, and gestured helplessly with her hands. 'I don't know how to thank you all.'

'Don't try,' Alex smiled warmly, placing Dale's glass of champagne in her hand. 'Let's drink once again to your future, and we wish you success in whatever you plan to do.'

'We echo that,' everyone murmured, and it was during the brief ensuing silence, while they all sipped at their champagne, that Dale became aware of Rick's strong arm about her waist, and the sinewy hardness of his body against her own. It felt so right standing there next to him, but her heart was suddenly beating much too fast, and she was beginning to realise that Tony was not the only one who was observing her and Rick with a curious expression in his eyes. Brenda Crawford and Alex were watching her too, and so was Joe, and when Dale darted a nervous glance up at Rick she could have sworn that she glimpsed a tender light

in his eyes before his familiar mask slipped into place. His arm fell away from her when she stirred against him, and the contact was broken, but her pulse was still behaving erratically as she resumed her seat and allowed Tony to fill up her glass.

The atmosphere was strangely tense, but Alex suggested that it was time they helped themselves to the buffet dinner Sheena had prepared, and everyone seemed to relax again—everyone except Dale. What had they seen? she wondered anxiously. Had she perhaps dropped her guard for a moment to let them see how she felt about Rick? She became choked at the thought, and was tempted to run to the safety of her room, but she controlled this mad desire, and tried desperately to behave as if nothing untowards had occurred.

Dale had only a few moments alone with Tony that evening when they stepped out on to the terrace, and for the first time there was a certain awkwardness between them which she did not understand until Tony said teasingly, 'Your guardian seems to behave a little possessively, don't you think?'

'I don't know what you mean,' she retorted stiffly, her startled glance meeting his.

'The way he held you and looked at you earlier was possessive, to say the least,' Tony insisted, and her eyes widened with mingled shock and dismay.

'Don't be ridiculous!'

'You didn't see the way he looked at you,' Tony laughed softly. 'His manner said clearly, "She's my property, and don't anyone forget it".'

'You're imagining things, Tony.'

He shrugged carelessly. 'Have it your way, but I wasn't the only one who noticed it.'

Dale felt again that suffocating, almost frantic desire to run. What would she be running from? she asked herself sensibly. From Rick's possessiveness, as Tony

and the others had seen it? Or her own crazy desire to be possessed?

'How do you feel about your father marrying Alex?' she changed the subject hastily.

'I think it's great!' he replied enthusiastically, leaning against the low wall and smiling at her. 'I've never seen my father this relaxed and happy before.'

'I feel they're so right for each other, and I just know they're going to be happy together.'

She raised her eyes to the stars and felt certain they echoed her sentiments, but something about Tony made her glance at him quickly. He shuffled his feet uncomfortably, and seemed to take a great interest in the carved pillar before he obviously found the courage to voice his troubled thoughts.

'Dale, there's something I want to tell you. We've known each other for some months now, and I guess you could say we know each other pretty well after all the letters we wrote to each other while I was doing my military training.' His hand found hers and gripped it firmly. 'You know I wouldn't want to do anything to hurt you.'

'What is it, Tony?'

'I've met a girl, and——'

'And you don't want me to feel bad if I don't see you so often in future,' she filled in for him when he paused awkwardly.

'You're not mad at me?'

'No, of course not,' she said gravely. 'I'd like to think you'll bring her round to my flat some time so that we could become friends as well.'

'Thank you for being so understanding,' he sighed, looking instantly relieved, then he released her hand as they went inside to join the others.

It was almost midnight when Joe and Tony left, and Dale was sitting next to Brenda Crawford when the older woman turned to her with a smile. 'Alex tells me

you've found yourself a flat.'

'What's this about a flat?' Rick intervened abruptly as he came in from the darkened terrace.

Dale looked up into that stern face with the angry eyes and hard, unrelenting jaw, and felt her insides quake, but she was not going to be intimidated on this occasion.

'I'm moving into a flat on the beachfront next week,' she explained, a glimmer of defiance in her unwavering glance.

'As I recall, I placed the cottage down at Ramsgate at your disposal, and at that time you seemed to like the idea,' he reminded her accusingly, his dark brows meeting in an angry frown above his eyes.

Dale moved her shoulders uncomfortably beneath the gathered folds of her cream-coloured silk evening dress. 'I know, and I appreciate your offer, but——'

'But you would really much prefer a place of your own,' Brenda Crawford filled in for Dale when she paused abruptly. 'Isn't that so, my dear?'

'Yes,' Dale nodded, glancing warily from Mrs Crawford's smiling, gentle face up into Rick's harsh, disapproving features. 'Oh, please! Try to understand, Rick.'

His mouth twisted derisively as he leaned against the ornamental fireplace. 'You want to spread your wings and fly a little?'

'Don't mock her, Rick,' Alex intervened for the first time to reprimand her brother. 'Dale is perfectly entitled to make her own decisions now that she's twenty-one.'

'That's quite true, of course,' Rick admitted readily.

'But you don't approve,' Dale voiced what she felt certain he had wanted to add.

'I'm disappointed, my little moonflower,' he corrected suavely, and a little mockingly. 'I foolishly thought the cottage would be a perfect setting for you,

but Alex is right—you're now entitled to make your own decisions.'

An awkward, strangely tense silence hovered in the room, but Brenda Crawford finally broke it when she rose to her feet and stifled a yawn. 'It's been a wonderful evening, but I think it's time we all went to bed.'

'I agree with you, Mother,' Alex said at once, rising briskly from her comfortable chair. 'Come on, Dale. It's been a long day.'

They went upstairs and said goodnight, but Dale could not go to sleep. *Moonflower*. Rick had called her *moonflower*, and her feeling of independence had melted away to awaken again that forbidden longing for something which she could never have. The pain of it seemed to gnaw away at her insides until she felt she could bear it no longer and, restless to the extreme, she finally pulled on her silk robe, and pushed her feet into soft mules. A glass of hot milk and fresh air nearly always helped to induce sleep on these occasions, and taking care not to wake the others in the house, she went down to the kitchen.

Dale stood out on the darkened terrace while she drank her milk. The air was warm and tranquil, and she was trying desperately to absorb some of that tranquillity into her mind and her soul. What she needed at that moment was the peace of the chapel at St Stephen's, for somehow it felt as if she would never have peace in her heart again.

The sound of a step behind her made her swing round sharply to see Rick emerging from the living-room. He had shed his jacket and tie, but his white shirt clung to the top half of his body to accentuate the width of his shoulders.

'Do you realise it's after one o'clock in the morning?' he demanded in his deep voice which never failed to stir her senses.

'I couldn't sleep.'

'Too much excitement?'

'Something like that,' she replied stiffly, hating the sound of mockery she detected in his voice as she placed her empty glass on the cane table beside her.

'The next celebration will be Alex's wedding,' he observed drily.

'Yes,' she murmured absently. 'Joe has been very patient.'

'So have I,' he said, leaning against the wall beside her and folding his arms across his chest.

He was referring to Melissa, of course, and Dale had no doubt about that as she asked with a forced casualness, 'Where's Miss Arnell?'

'She's modelling in Cape Town at the moment.'

That explained it, she thought miserably. 'When do you expect her back?'

'I have no idea at all when she's returning to Durban,' he answered her with a certain amount of impatience, then he changed the subject abruptly. 'I would appreciate an hour of your time tomorrow. There are several things I must bring to your attention concerning your inheritance.'

His tone was authoritative and commanding, and she said hastily, 'I haven't planned anything for tomorrow.'

'Good,' he said abruptly. 'We'll schedule the discussion for after breakfast, then, and get it over and done with.'

Hurt, and vaguely annoyed by his autocratic manner, she whispered mockingly, 'Yes, *sir*.'

'Don't call me that!' he barked at her, and the harshness in his voice sent an icy chill sweeping through her.

'I'm sorry,' she gulped, turning from him, but his fingers snaked about her wrist to prevent her from

leaving, and when he had captured both her wrists he drew her up against him until she could feel the hard muscles of his thighs against her own. She was afraid and excited simultaneously by this unexpected contact with his body, and every instinct warned her to escape, but to struggle in his grip would merely infuriate him, and she dared not risk the consequences.

'I'm the one who should apologise,' he said softly, gazing down into her pale face. 'I've had a trying week, and I'm a little ratty, but that's no reason why I should take it out on you.'

Her breathing felt too restricted to speak, and she was horrifyingly sure Rick must be able to feel her pulses racing beneath his fingertips against her wrists. She tried to read his expression, but his face was shadowed, and for interminable seconds she toyed with the temptation to lean her weary head against his solid chest. She might have swayed a little closer to him, she could not be sure, but the barely perceptible tightening of his fingers about her wrists had the effect of a warning, and she came rapidly to her senses.

'I think I'd like to go up to my room now,' she forced the words past her stiff lips, and he released her instantly. She stepped away from him, feeling lightheaded and shaky on her legs, then she turned and fled without another word.

In Alex's study the following morning, Rick explained to Dale in detail the extent of her inheritance. She was, as he had once said, a very wealthy young woman, but she viewed her inheritance with very little interest.

'I've drawn up a few documents which are basically for your own protection as a shareholder in your late father's business, and I would like you to study them carefully before you sign them,' Rick informed her in

a businesslike manner, producing the documents from his briefcase and placing them in her hands.

Dale stared at the legal documents and felt a little sick inside. 'I don't think I want to read them.'

'You can't sign your name to something you haven't read,' he reminded her mockingly. 'It's bad policy.'

'You've always taken adequate care of my business affairs, and I see no reason why I shouldn't trust you now,' she argued stubbornly. 'If you would lend me your pen, then I will sign these and be done with it.'

'As your attorney I consider it my duty to point out that you should never sign any document, legal or otherwise, without first scrutinising the contents.'

'You told me you'd drawn up these documents for my protection as a shareholder, and that's more than I need to know,' she replied distastefully, taking the pen he held out to her, and signing the papers where he had indicated with pencil crosses. When it was done, she pushed the documents and the pen back at him across the desk. 'Was there anything else?'

'Yes,' he said abruptly, getting up and walking round to Dale's side to seat himself on the corner of the desk. 'Your liquid assets have been invested for you in various reputable companies, as you'll see from this list.' He thrust a sheet of paper at her, and when she took it from him she turned and walked across to the window without so much as a glance at the names of the companies which had been so carefully listed. She was overwhelmed by everything he had told her, but she was also sad, and so many images from the past flashed through her mind as Rick continued speaking. 'The dividends alone will provide you with a sizeable income, but then there's still your monthly income from the business.' He paused abruptly and, crossing the room to her side, he demanded sharply, 'Are you listening to me, Dale?'

'Yes, I'm listening, and I'm thinking about all those

years I'd been forced to survive on close to nothing.' She sighed and continued to stare fixedly out of the window at the starlings feeding and caring for their young in a way she had never been cared for by the two people whom she had thought were her parents. 'I never understood it then, but I do now, and the bitterness of those years has been replaced by a feeling of humility.'

'Humility?' Rick asked, turning her to face him, and she gestured expressively with the hand that held the list containing the names of companies in which she now had money invested.

'I don't deserve all this.'

'You were Ivan and Celeste's only child,' he kept up the pretence smoothly, and she would never have doubted him if she had not by chance discovered the truth. 'That makes you eligible, I would say.'

'Rick, I——' She bit back the burning confession. She despised Rick's deceit as well as her own, but this was not the time to confront him with what she knew. She felt his eyes on her lowered face, watching, waiting, and she said lamely, 'I suppose you're right.'

Rick did not pursue the subject, and she was grateful for that, but she knew that there would come a time when she would have to admit to reading that letter Ivan Palmer had written to him. It was something she did not look forward to, but it was something which she knew would have to be done if she was to live with her conscience in future.

His knuckles brushed lightly against her cheek. 'Don't you think it's time you took me to see your flat?'

'So that you can put your stamp of approval on it?' she teased.

'Now, Dale,' he rebuked her lightly. 'Because I'm no longer your guardian it doesn't mean that I no longer have an interest in your welfare.'

Her blue eyes were grave as she raised them to his. 'I'd like to thank you, Rick, for accepting the responsibility my—my father foisted on to you, and for taking me into your home. I shall always be grateful for your kindness and your concern.'

'It sounds almost as if you're saying goodbye,' he mocked her.

'In a way I am,' she admitted, folding the sheet of paper absently between her trembling fingers. 'I'm saying goodbye to the old life, and starting a new one.'

'Will there still be a place for the Crawfords in this new life of yours, I wonder?'

'There will always be a place for you,' she said at once, and the words came from her heart in not quite the sense he had meant it. *There will always be a place for you in my heart, even though I know there will never be a place in yours for me.*

They drove down to the beachfront in Dale's Golf a few minutes later, leaving Alex and Mrs Crawford tentatively discussing the arrangements for Alex's wedding. Dale's mind went back to that day when Rick had brought the Golf to his home, and had insisted that they go for a drive so that he could observe her skill as a driver. That was almost two years ago, and she had scarcely known Rick then, yet at that precise moment it felt as if she had known him all her life.

Dale drove down into the basement of a white-washed building and parked her car in the space alotted to her. She felt nervous suddenly, and unsure of herself. Had she done the right thing? But, more to the point, would Rick think so?

'I was lucky to get this flat,' she said simply to ease the awkward silence between them as the lift swept them up to the fifteenth floor. 'It went vacant unexpectedly, and I came along just at the right moment.'

'So it seems,' Rick answered abruptly, and once again that dreadful silence descended between them, and it lingered until she finally unlocked the door to her flat and took him inside.

Their steps echoed hollowly in the empty rooms as she took him on a tour of what would very soon be her home, and her heart seemed to beat just as hollowly against her ribs when they eventually stood facing each other in the lounge. Rick had said very little, and his expression had given away even less, but she was not going to be swayed on this matter.

'Is this really what you want?' he asked at length, his eyes narrowed and intent upon her raised face.

'Yes, this is what I want.'

He nodded slowly and cast a swift, appraising glance about the room. 'I shall look forward to seeing it when it's furnished.'

It was only as she expelled the air from her lungs that she realised she had been holding her breath, and a smile lifted the corners of her mouth. 'You approve?'

'You have an excellent view of the sea, and the rooms are spacious and airy,' he replied with a hint of laughter in his dark eyes. 'What more could anyone want?'

'I'm happy to know you feel that way about it.'

Rick thrust his hands into his pockets and observed her through narrowed eyes that glittered strangely. 'It doesn't take much to make you happy, does it?'

'I suppose not,' she agreed soberly. 'I've never expected, nor asked for much, and I've been happy with what I've had.'

'You don't regret living most of your life with the nuns at the Academy?'

'I don't regret it, and I learnt a lot from Sister Teresa,' she replied almost defensively.

'Spiritually you may have learnt a lot, yes,' he agreed. 'But what did she teach you about life itself?'

'What do you mean?' she asked warily.

'Did the good Sister Teresa prepare you at all for the wicked world beyond the Academy walls?' he wanted to know, his smile twisted with mockery, and she was instantly on her guard.

'I think I know all I need to know.'

'Do you?'

'I'm twenty-one, Rick,' she pointed out coolly, and a dangerous light leapt into his dark eyes.

'So you are,' he drawled.

Her fingers fumbled nervously with the small bunch of keys in her hand, but her voice was cool and distant when she said, 'I think we should end this conversation and leave.'

'There are times when I think you positively dislike me, and this is one of them,' Rick observed drily as she turned resolutely towards the door, and she paused abruptly with her back turned towards him.

'I don't dislike you.'

'What is it, then?' he demanded harshly, his hand heavy on her shoulder as he spun her round to face him. 'What makes you withdraw into that shell of yours like a scared tortoise whenever I start digging beneath the surface of that cool and calm exterior of yours?'

Dale felt compelled to meet his dark, probing eyes, but somehow she found the strength to brush off his query lightly. 'Perhaps I'm afraid you'll discover there's nothing there beneath the shell.'

'You're not an empty vessel, Dale,' he argued with angry impatience. 'You're as deep as the ocean, and some day I'm going to succeed in my efforts to delve right beneath that calm surface.'

Panic coiled through her, but she tried to laugh it off. 'That sounds almost like a threat!'

'It's a promise,' he corrected, and a chill of apprehension spiralled through her as he released her

shoulder and crossed the room to open the door. 'Let's go.'

Dale drove back to Alex's home in silence, and neither did Rick make an attempt to speak. There was once again that tension between them which she could not understand, and she did not have another opportunity to speak to him privately before he and his mother returned to Durban after lunch.

Joe joined Alex and Dale for dinner that evening, and afterwards, when they sat out on the terrace, Alex turned to Dale. 'You might like to know it's all been decided. Joe and I are getting married this coming Saturday.'

'Oh, I'm so glad!' Dale smiled across at the two people sitting so close together on the bench, then a thought leapt into her mind. 'That doesn't give us much time to prepare.'

'There isn't much to prepare,' Alex assured her calmly. 'It's going to be a very quiet wedding with only my mother, Rick, Tony, and yourself to wish us well, and afterwards . . .'

'And afterwards,' Joe picked up the thread of Alex's explanation while he puffed contentedly at his pipe. 'Afterwards I'll treat you all to a champagne lunch at the hotel before Alex and I hitch up my caravan and take off into the wilderness for a few weeks.'

'That sounds marvellous,' Dale sighed, envying them quite suddenly. 'Are you going to be away long?'

'Our time is our own,' Joe grinned, his teeth clenched on the stem of his favourite pipe. 'It might be two weeks, or it might be six. It all depends on how soon we get tired of travelling about.'

'I'm a bit worried about you, though,' Alex announced, glancing at Dale with concern.

'Please don't worry about me,' Dale said hastily. 'I shall have moved into my flat, and I shall be terribly busy getting everything sorted out the way I want it.'

'You know, of course, that you can depend on Rick for any assistance you might require,' Alex reminded her, and Dale nodded.

'Yes, I know.'

'And there's Tony too,' Joe intervened. 'Don't forget that.'

'I shan't forget,' Dale promised.

The week that followed was an exceptionally busy one for both Alex and Dale. While Alex made frantic preparations for her wedding, Dale was involved in furnishing her flat and having curtains made, and before either of them realised it, it was Saturday morning.

Rick and Mrs Crawford arrived two hours before the noon wedding, and while Rick went off to keep Joe company at his home, Mrs Crawford and Dale remained with Alex to help her dress and pack the last-minute things for her honeymoon.

Alex looked chic and incredibly calm, but Dale sensed that underneath that calm exterior the happiness and excitement were building up to almost a fever pitch. Would I feel like this on my wedding day? Dale wondered absently as she studied Alex's slim figure in the ivory-coloured outfit she had chosen for her wedding day. Her thoughts came to an abrupt halt. There would be no wedding bells for her. She dared not risk placing the burden of her heritage on any man. It would be unfair, and quite unthinkable.

Alex and Joe were married in church, a brief, holy ceremony which bound them together for life, and Dale felt the sting of happy tears behind her eyes as she sat silently in the pew watching the proceedings. Rick was sitting beside her, his thigh almost brushing against hers as she glanced at him surreptitiously, but he was staring straight ahead, his strong profile etched against the stained glass window. What was he

thinking? Was he remembering, perhaps, how close he had once come to marriage, or was he wishing that Melissa would agree some day to marry him? The thought of Rick marrying Melissa Arnell was abhorrent, but it was one which Dale would have to accept and learn to live with.

As Joe had promised, he treated them all to an elaborate champagne luncheon at the hotel, and when they finally waved goodbye and set off on their honeymoon, they left four silent people standing on the pavement outside the hotel. Tony excused himself soon afterwards, and that left three; Brenda Crawford, Rick, and Dale.

'I do hope they're going to be happy,' Mrs Crawford sighed, dabbing lightly at her eyes with her lace handkerchief.

'Naturally they're going to be happy, Mother,' Rick said almost impatiently. 'Joe is the right man for Alex. He'll handle her gently but firmly, and the latter is what she quite often needs.'

'You're right, of course,' Brenda agreed with her son, but the tears were still very close.

'What about coming to my flat for a cup of coffee before you return home?' Dale changed the subject, and Brenda's face brightened at once.

'I was hoping you'd suggest that, my dear,' she smiled. 'I'm terribly inquisitive to see where you're going to stay.'

Dale glanced questioningly at Rick, and he nodded his approval abruptly, but remained silent.

A few moments later Dale was driving ahead in her Golf while Rick followed with Mrs Crawford in his Mercedes. In the rear-view mirror she could see his stern features behind the wheel of his car, and once again she found herself wondering what he had been thinking about in church during the marriage ceremony. She wished suddenly that she had known

him all those years ago. Perhaps he had smiled more often instead of always looking so stern, but then he would have had so much more to smile about. He had been in love with an intelligent young woman, but fate had taken her from him so cruelly. With Melissa it was different, Dale decided. It could only be a physical thing between them, for Dale felt certain that Rick would never love again. Alex had called him stone-hearted, and Dale found herself agreeing with that description.

She collected her thoughts sharply when they arrived at the whitewashed building where she had now made her home, and a few minutes later she was ushering Mrs Crawford and Rick into her flat.

'Oh, but this is very nice,' Brenda exclaimed, casting her glance over the cool appearance of the tastefully furnished lounge with its comfortably padded chairs, and décor in soothing autumn shades. 'And what an incredibly lovely view,' she added sincerely, walking across to the window, and her footsteps made no sound on the thick carpet with its leafy pattern of green and gold.

'What do you think?' Dale asked directly, glancing up at Rick, and his hard mouth twisted into a semblance of a smile.

'There's certainly a vast improvement since the last time I saw it.'

'I should imagine there is,' she agreed, hiding her nervousness behind a careless laugh. 'This time I can at least offer you a chair to sit on, and make you something to drink.'

Brenda Crawford was not content with seeing only the lounge, and Dale took her from room to room before she switched on the kettle and made the coffee.

They left an hour later, and only then did Dale take stock of her position. She was on her own now. She was twenty-one, and mistress of her own fate, and all

at once she felt incredibly lonely. As much as she had always enjoyed being on her own, just as much she hated that thought now. Being alone meant being with one's own thoughts, and her thoughts of late were like a moth helplessly circling the flame of a candle. Rick had become the axle around which her life pivoted. She thought of him first thing in the morning, and last thing at night, and during the day it had become a deathly struggle to shut him out of her mind and her heart. She succeeded sometimes in shutting him out of her mind, but she never quite succeeded in shutting him out of her heart. Without realising it, Rick had taken possession; he had invaded the sanctum of her soul, and nothing, it seemed, would thrust him out.

CHAPTER NINE

DALE'S life took on a complete new dimension during those four weeks while Alex and Joe were on their honeymoon. She sketched and painted, and went for long walks in search of new material, and on one occasion she packed her gear into the Golf and spent a few days exploring the northern part of Natal. She was sketching the countryside with its rolling hills, its sugar cane and timber plantations. There was also time to sketch the palms, wild strelitzias, and flame trees, and she loved every minute of this new adventure.

She felt free, in a sense, but Rick was always there, acting as a reminder that a part of her would never be entirely free of him. He called on her regularly twice a week, driving down from Durban in the evenings, and a weekend seldom passed that he did not arrive on her doorstep with an invitation to spend the day with him somewhere along the lush Natal coast. Other than that he seemed content to accompany her on her long walks, and then he would simply sit somewhere quietly when she found something worth sketching.

This new relationship between Rick and herself often puzzled her. It was easy and relaxed, as if they were getting to know each other all over again, but she sometimes got the feeling that a storm was brewing beneath the calm surface, and it frequently unnerved her.

Rick took her down to Ramsgate one Sunday afternoon and when they approached the cottage he said: 'Close your eyes, I have a surprise for you.'

She obeyed, and only when he had helped her out of the car was she allowed to open her eyes.

The cottage, completed, nestled attractively among the trees with its whitewashed walls and cool thatched roof, but her glance was drawn irresistibly towards a brass name plate against the wall beside the entrance.

Little Eden.

It was the name she had secretly given it, and her heart leapt into her throat. 'How—How did you know?'

'Come inside and I'll explain.'

Dale felt choked, and the blood in her veins turned to ice as they went into the cottage and walked through each of the rooms. She ought to have been overjoyed, but instead it felt as if she had walked into a nightmare. The cottage had been furnished exactly as she had envisaged it in her sketches. It was all there in the décor, down to the minutest detail, and she could not bear to look at Rick when he explained.

'Sheena found your sketches in the waste basket beside your desk. She wasn't sure what to do with them, and passed them on to Alex.'

'And Alex showed them to you,' Dale concluded dully.

'She suspected it had something to do with the cottage,' Rick admitted. 'I liked your sketches, so I passed them on to an interior decorator as soon as the cottage was completed.'

'And the name? How did you guess I'd named it "Little Eden"?'

'There was no guesswork involved,' Rick laughed shortly, and the sound jarred her nerves. 'You'd printed the name in a corner of one of your sketches.'

'I wasn't aware of that.'

He turned her to face him, and his eyes probed her rigid features. 'I thought you'd be surprised and pleased.'

'I am surprised,' she admitted reluctantly. 'But what about Melissa? What if she doesn't like it?'

His jaw hardened. 'Must you always be so concerned about Melissa?'

'There are times when I simply don't understand you,' she confessed with some annoyance.

'There are times when you infuriate me beyond reason, and this is one of them,' he countered harshly.

It was a disastrous outing, and they drove back to Amanzimtoti in silence. If Rick had wanted to hurt her, then he had succeeded admirably. He had taken her very personal dream of 'Little Eden', but he was making Melissa Arnell mistress of it, and she could almost hate him for doing this to her.

Alex called round to see Dale on the morning after their return from their honeymoon, and she looked tanned, happy, and relaxed in a way Dale had never seen her before.

'We've got a problem,' Alex explained laughingly when Dale asked where they would be making their home. 'I don't want to move into Joe's house, and he doesn't fancy moving into mine.'

'I imagine he's concerned about what people might say,' Dale observed shrewdly.

'He is,' Alex agreed ruefully, 'but I think I've found the solution.'

'And that is?' Dale prompted, pouring out the tea and passing Alex a cup.

'We'll stay at my place for the time being, but we'll sell up everything as soon as we can, and buy a place together.'

'Have you decided where you want to buy?'

'That's another problem,' Alex announced. 'We fancy a place along the north coast where it still looks wild and beautiful, and untouched by man.'

Dale looked bewildered. 'Where's the problem in that?'

'I'm concerned about you.'

'Oh, nonsense, Alex,' Dale laughed. 'I'm perfectly

happy here, and you're not to let me stand in the way of what you and Joe want.'

'I happen to be very fond of you.'

'Oh, Alex . . .' A warmth invaded Dale's heart as their glances met. 'I'm fond of you too, but I'd hate to become an obstacle in the path of your happiness.'

A lump rose in Dale's throat at the unexpected sight of tears glistening in Alex's eyes, but Alex blinked them away hastily, and changed the subject. 'Have you seen much of Rick lately?'

Dale was instantly on her guard. The pain of her last meeting with Rick was still much too raw, and she said vaguely, 'I see him occasionally.'

'Is Melissa still very much in the picture?'

'Rick never discusses her with me,' Dale replied truthfully, and Alex gestured disparagingly.

'I hope to goodness he isn't fool enough to marry that woman.'

Dale could not help agreeing with her, but she decided it would be safer not to discuss something which really did not concern her.

'More tea?' she asked, gesturing towards the tea-pot.

'No, I must rush,' Alex declined, draining her cup hastily and picking up her shopping bag on the way out. 'Come and see us any time you feel like company.'

'I'll do that,' Dale promised, and moments later Alex was making a dash for one of the descending lifts.

Dale felt vaguely disturbed after that. Why should Alex question her about Melissa? It was puzzling, but she soon thrust it from her mind when she settled down to work in front of her easel. The smell of paint and turps hovered in the room she had turned into a studio of sorts, but she barely noticed it as she concentrated on capturing the restless sea on canvas.

That afternoon, however, it was very much a case of 'speak of the devil'. The ringing of the doorbell forced

her to relinquish her work, and she was rendered momentarily speechless when she found Melissa Arnell on her doorstep. Beautiful and elegant in a white, strapless dress with emerald green beads slung carelessly yet attractively about her slender throat, she slid her derisive glance down the length of Dale, taking in her faded blue jeans and paint-soiled smock.

'Aren't you going to invite me in?' she smiled condescendingly.

'Yes, of course,' Dale muttered apologetically, Melissa's perfume quivering offensively in her nostrils as she opened the door wider. 'Come in.'

Melissa stepped past Dale, and her cold grey eyes swept the room briefly. 'My, what a nice little place you have here!'

Dale was not fooled into believing that this woman had paid her a friendly visit, and as she gestured Melissa into a chair, she said quietly but firmly, 'I'm sure you didn't come here to admire my flat, Miss Arnell.'

'How very astute of you, my dear,' Melissa observed in her musical voice, and crossed her shapely legs very elegantly while Dale lowered herself gingerly on to the padded arm of the vacant chair behind her. 'I came to talk to you about Rick.'

Dale should have expected something like this, but somehow she had never given it a thought, and a ghastly coldness invaded her rigid body as she sat there facing the beautiful Melissa Arnell.

'What about Rick?' she somehow managed to ask in a voice that betrayed none of her feelings.

'I've thought for some time that someone ought to enlighten you, but as no one else will do so, I've taken the task upon myself.'

A child's laughter in the corridor outside shattered the uneasy silence in the room. 'Say what you have to

say, and get it over with,' Dale instructed in a clipped voice.

'Very well,' Melissa smiled mirthlessly. 'You and Rick have been seeing rather a lot of each other lately.'

'I don't deny that.'

'Have you stopped to ask yourself why?'

'Not that I can recall,' Dale replied, wondering what this was leading up to, but she did not have long to wait for the answer.

'Rick still considers himself responsible for your welfare, darling, and for some ridiculous reason he feels sorry for you.'

'Sorry for me?' Dale echoed incredulously, experiencing the sensation that something distasteful had entered her mouth.

'You surely didn't imagine he could care for you in any other way, did you?' Melissa laughed unkindly, hitting at Dale's most vulnerable area. 'My dear, you simply have to look in the mirror to find the answer to that!'

Dale got jerkily to her feet and turned from Melissa to hide the pain in her eyes. 'I've never been foolish enough to think that Rick could care for me in any special way, but I did begin to think of him as a friend, instead of the man who used to be my guardian.'

'Don't be so naïve, darling,' Melissa's laughter flayed her again. 'It certainly isn't friendship that brings Rick here so often. It's his outsize sense of responsibility and his pity for you that makes him dog your doorstep, and don't be mistaken about that.'

Pity! The word jabbed at Dale's pride and sliced into her soul like a hot knife through butter, but nothing on earth would induce her to let this woman see how much she had hurt her, and she clung to her crumbling composure as she turned to face Melissa.

'Was there anything else you had to tell me?' she

asked coldly, seeing the light of triumph in those grey, heavily-lashed eyes.

'I've said what I came to say,' Melissa announced, rising to her feet in a practised, fluid motion. 'I'll leave the rest up to you.'

Dale stood frozen while Melissa let herself out. She could not recall afterwards how long she had stood there before she realised that she was shaking as if with a fever, while hot tears slid unheeded down her pale cheeks. She felt humiliated, hurt and insulted, and when she could not stop the tears from flowing, she sat down in the nearest chair and simply cried until she had no more tears left to shed.

She tried to convince herself that Melissa had said all those things merely to hurt her, but she failed miserably. Melissa had not said much that Dale had not known or suspected for a long time. She had simply underlined certain things as well as adding a few, and if it was true that no one else had had the heart to enlighten Dale, then Melissa had been the ideal emissary. She had had all the weapons with which to fire those painful darts—and she had Rick too.

Dale went through to the bathroom and splashed cold water onto her hot face, and when she had dabbed it dry with a towel she stared at herself in the mirror above the basin. There was nothing even remotely attractive about her face at that moment, she decided in a fit of unnecessary cruelty towards herself. Her eyes were red and the lids were swollen, and her wide, soft mouth quivered with the effort not to burst into tears again.

'God, help me!' she prayed aloud, pressing the towel against the mirror to blot out her image, and leaning her weary head against it until she regained her composure sufficiently to go through to the kitchen to make herself a cup of strong tea.

'I'll leave the rest up to you,' Melissa had said.

'Well, if it is up to me,' Dale spoke her thoughts aloud, 'then the sooner I do something about it, the better.'

It was futile thinking she could concentrate on painting again that afternoon, so she went for a long walk instead to prepare herself mentally for her confrontation with Rick that evening. She knew he would come, he nearly always drove down to see her on a Tuesday evening, and she wanted to be ready for him when he arrived. *Pity!* Each time that word shot through her mind it pierced her to her very soul, and she finally resorted to anger as her only defence against the pain. When she returned to her flat she stormed about for a while in a totally uncharacteristic manner, picking up this, and slamming down that as she gave vent to her feelings, but she realised eventually that her anger would be futile against Rick's logical, lawyer's mind. If she wanted to cope with the task ahead of her, she would have to compose herself, and she did so with difficulty during the time still alotted to her.

Dale was outwardly calm and poised that evening when her doorbell rang, but inwardly she was a nervous wreck. Her hands were shaking and her throat felt tight, but she paused only for a moment to draw a steadying breath before she unlocked the door.

'Hello, Rick,' she said without her usual welcoming smile as she opened the door wider to admit his tall, imposing figure. 'Please come in, and sit down.'

'I could do with a cup of coffee,' he sighed, loosening his sober tie and discarding the jacket of his dark grey suit before he lowered himself tiredly into one of her comfortable chairs.

He looked so utterly exhausted that her tender heart weakened for one brief moment, but then she remembered what she had to do, and pulled herself together sharply.

'I'll switch the kettle on,' she said as she turned

towards the kitchen, and while she waited for the water to boil she primed herself severely for what she knew had to follow.

Rick lay sprawled in his chair with his eyes shut when she returned to the lounge a few minutes later, and she thought for a moment that he was asleep, but he opened his eyes and sat up with a grunt when she placed his cup of coffee on the low table beside his chair.

'You're looking a little pale,' he observed while they drank their coffee, and his dark eyes studied her intently. 'Aren't you feeling well?'

'I'm perfectly all right, thank you.'

'You don't look all right to me.' He put down his cup and frowned. 'Come to think of it, you don't sound right either.'

Scraping together the fragments of her courage, she met the onslaught of his dark, probing glance. 'Rick, I want to talk to you.'

'Ah, so there *is* something,' he smiled twistedly, and she imagined that this was how he looked in the courtroom when he had had his suspicions confirmed. 'What is it?' he asked abruptly.

'I want you to know that I'm quite happy and contented here where I am, and that there's no need for you to feel you still have a responsibility towards me,' she rattled off her well-rehearsed speech, only now it did not sound quite so convincing to her own ears. 'I can take care of myself,' she added for good measure.

Rick's eyes narrowed as he sat forward in his chair and rested his elbows on his knees. 'I have a feeling there's something more to this announcement than simply the need to remind me that you're now totally independent.'

Her cup rattled in its saucer and, avoiding his penetrating gaze, she put it down hastily. 'I would prefer it if you refrained from coming here so often in future.'

'I see,' he drawled mockingly. 'You want our relationship to continue on a purely business level, is that it?'

'I would prefer it that way.'

'Why?' he shot the question at her after a frightening little silence, and Dale jumped to her feet to put some distance between them.

'I've already explained,' she said, staring blindly through the open window down on to the dark, deserted beach.

'No, you haven't,' Rick spoke sharply behind her, and his hands bit cruelly into her shoulders as he turned her roughly to face him. 'You've stressed the well known fact that you're now an independent young woman who is capable of taking care of herself, but you haven't told me *why* I am no longer welcome here as a friend.'

Anger and pain rose like the tide within her until the truth was wrenched from her lips. 'I don't want your pity, Rick!'

'*Pity?*' he demanded harshly, releasing her so abruptly that she swayed momentarily and had to lean against the windowsill for support. 'Who said anything about pity?'

She swallowed convulsively. 'There's no need for you to pretend.'

'So now I'm pretending, am I?'

'You *know* you are.'

His eyes darkened with a savage fury that made her shrink from him in fear as he demanded in a thundering voice, 'Since when have I ever pitied you?'

'I suspect you—you always have,' she managed haltingly, not understanding his terrible anger as he towered over her menacingly.

Dale, I could throttle you!' he growled, his dark eyes stabbing at her like twin fires, and his hands actually circling her slender throat, then he released

her abruptly with a muttered oath and walked a few paces away from her, almost as if he could not bear to be near her. Shaking from head to foot, she closed her eyes and willed him to leave, but his lawyer's mind was not yet satisfied. 'Someone has put this crazy idea into your head, and I want to know who it is.'

'Won't you please go, Rick?' she pleaded tiredly, staring at his formidable back as he stooped to retrieve something which had lodged itself between the cushion and the armrest of the chair he had sat in.

'Was it Melissa?' he flung the question at her, and her face went a shade whiter.

'No, it was not.'

'You're lying, Dale,' he accused in a frighteningly calm voice as he turned slowly to face her, and from his strong fingers there dangled a square of fine linen of the kind Melissa always carried with her. 'I'll ask you that question again. Was it Melissa?'

Dale stared at the handkerchief and knew what it must feel like to be in the witness-box and faced with such damning evidence. She had not seen the handkerchief lodged in the chair, and she felt certain Melissa would curse herself at this moment if she knew where she had lost it, but this was not the time to think of that. Rick was waiting for an answer to his query with the patience of an attorney who knew that he had his witness firmly in a corner, and she could no longer lie when she looked up into his piercingly angry eyes.

'Yes,' she whispered in a choked voice, 'It was Melissa.'

'She was here this afternoon?'

'Yes.'

'And she told you I pitied you?'

'She said you felt sorry for me,' Dale used the words Melissa had uttered, and quite suddenly she was afraid for the woman who had hurt her so deeply.

'Oh, Rick, don't hold it against her. She simply considered it was her duty to tell me the truth,' she pleaded, raising her hands imploringly as she lessened the distance between them.

'The truth?' he snapped as he pocketed the handkerchief. 'You accepted that from her as the truth?'

The lash of his voice made her step a pace away from him again and, taking a deep breath to calm herself, she asked: 'Why would she lie to me, and why else would you come here so often if it's not because you consider you still have certain obligations towards my well-being?'

His features tightened menacingly. 'I'll leave you to figure that out for yourself,' he snarled, 'and while you're doing that you might as well attempt to figure this out too.'

His hands shot out, and before she had time to guess his intentions she was crushed against the hard length of his body. His mouth came down on hers, stifling her cry of protest, and claiming her lips with a savagery that frightened and bewildered her. She tried to struggle free, but her arms were pinned at her sides, and he did not release her until an unwilling response shuddered through her.

Free of his arms, she swayed dizzily and, through a film of hot, stinging tears, she saw him pick up his jacket and stride out of her flat.

She felt sick and utterly lost, and her legs were shaking so much that she had to sit down. Why had the truth angered him so much? And why did it have to feel as if her entire world had suddenly crumbled about her?

Dale slept very little that night. She was restless and disturbed, and she spent most of the hours pacing her bedroom floor while her mind conjured up one bewildering question after the other for which she

could find no answer. Was it possible that Melissa could have lied? But with what purpose in mind? She had Rick; she had everything, so what more did she want? Had she perhaps said those things simply to cause hurt and humiliation? But why? Why? And why had Rick been so angry?

The battle that went on inside Dale lasted through the next few days and on into the weekend before she found an answer which troubled her even more than her queries. A woman like Melissa would only lie about something if she felt that she was being threatened in some way. Perhaps she suspected that Rick was directing his affections elsewhere, and this would naturally make her determined to eliminate the opposition. 'Am I the suspected opposition?' Dale wondered, and this thought alarmed her more than anything else. It lit a flame of hope which was forbidden, and she doused it swiftly, dismissing it as totally ridiculous. If Melissa imagined she might have opposition, then she would most certainly have to look elsewhere for the culprit.

Dale wandered down to the beach late that Saturday afternoon and, in that disturbed state of mind, she went swimming. The tide was high, and the waves came thrashing to the shore with a frightening force, but Dale was not afraid of the sea. She swam for a short while, surfing in the waves where the water was shallow, and she was totally unprepared for what eventually occurred. A wave broke over her head, knocking her off her feet and rolling her about like a piece of driftwood. She made a frantic attempt to get a foothold in the sand, but an incredibly strong backwash pulled her under, and when she finally surfaced she realised that she was several metres away from the shore. She dragged air into her tortured lungs and tried to ride the waves, hoping to reach the shore that way, but she succeeded only in drifting

farther out towards the shark nets. She was a strong swimmer, but fighting against the current was like fighting against a demon, and she merely exhausted herself.

'Don't panic, just stay afloat,' she warned herself repeatedly, but as the shoreline drifted farther away from her she began to know the real meaning of fear.

She could not recall afterwards whether minutes or hours had elapsed while she fought against the turbulent sea in an effort to stay afloat, but she had gone down several times and had swallowed a considerable amount of salty sea water before strong arms lifted her lifeless body almost from the ocean bed and helped her back to safety.

'Relax, Dale, I've got you, and you're quite safe,' Tony's reassuring voice burst through the roaring in her head, but her waterlogged lungs made her cough and splutter in reply.

She was only barely conscious when Tony carried her out of the sea on to the beach, and when he lowered her on to the sand she was vaguely aware of a strong, rhythmic pressure on her ribcage. It forced the water from her lungs, making her choke and gasp as it passed her lips, and she finally came to her senses to find Rick kneeling beside her on the sand.

'Dale, are you all right?' he questioned her harshly.

She had no idea where he had come from so unexpectedly, but she did not particularly care at that moment as she whispered weakly, 'Yes, I—I think so.'

'What in heaven's name happened?' Rich demanded, his face a curious grey as he straightened to confront Tony.

'The current was a little unpredictable today. We had a notice up prohibiting swimming, but she obviously didn't see it, and the current dragged her out to sea,' Tony explained, his chest still heaving from his recent exertion.

Rick nodded abruptly. 'Thanks for your help, Tony, and I appreciate your quick action.'

'That's okay,' Tony brushed his compliment aside, then he turned and ordered the inquisitive bystanders to disperse.

Dale felt ridiculously embarrassed as Rick kneeled down beside her again with a total disregard for his immaculate grey pants, and she found it almost impossible to meet his dark, probing glance.

'Rick, I—I'm sorry, I—I didn't mean to——'

'Where did you leave your towel and your robe?' he cut into her stammering apology, and his voice sounded unfamiliarly raw.

'Up there next to the wall,' she said, pointing in the general direction to where the showers were situated.

'Right,' he said abruptly, and the next instant she was being lifted in his arms like a child and carried up towards the grassy embankment.

Dale could not remember a time when she had ever been so acutely conscious of her appearance. Her blue one-piece swimsuit clung damply to her slender body, accentuating the gentle curve of her breasts and hips, and leaving very little to the imagination. Sand clung to her legs and arms, and knotted her hair, and the saltiness of the ocean was still nauseatingly in her mouth. Rick's arms were hard about her, and when she risked a glance at his face so close to her own, his grim expression filled her with a sense of foreboding.

He lowered her on to the wall and picked up her towel. Without speaking he brushed most of the sand off her arms and legs before he helped her into her robe and knotted the belt about her waist as if she was incapable of doing so herself.

'I—I can walk, Rick, truly I can,' she finally protested when he was about to lift her in his arms again, and he nodded abruptly.

'Let's go, then.'

His hand beneath her elbow supported her on legs that behaved like jelly, and her head felt as if it had been stuffed with cotton wool when they eventually reached her flat.

'I'll switch on the kettle and make some coffee while you shower and change,' he said without looking at her, but there was something about him that awakened a need in her to apologise once again.

'Rick, I——'

'Do as I say!' he cut in harshly, and when she stood there staring up at him rather helplessly, he gave her a gentle push in the direction of her bedroom.

Dale obeyed him automatically, and her embarrassment was intensified when she caught sight of herself in the dressing-table mirror. She looked a fright with her wet, sandy hair hanging about her white face like a stringy mop, and the knowledge that Rick had seen her looking like this made her dash into the bathroom with a choked cry of mortification on her lips.

She showered and washed her hair, and afterwards she stood for several minutes under the warm jet of water to ease away the ache in her body as well as the memory of those moments of terror when she had thought that she would be dragged down into the murky depths of the ocean. She had not seen the notice Tony had spoken of, and neither had she thought to indicate that she was in trouble. She had been too busy trying to keep afloat, and she could only think that providence had sent Tony out there to rescue her. She had not got around to thanking him for saving her life, but it was something she was determined to rectify as soon as possible.

She slipped on a floral silk dress which was cool and comfortable, dried her hair quickly with a blow-drier and brush, and applied make-up with a little more care than usual to her pale face. She was reluctant

somehow to confront Rick again, but there was no way she could escape it, and neither could she keep him waiting inside much longer.

Rick had the coffee waiting when she walked into the lounge, and she accepted a cup from him in silence. She avoided his eyes, but she felt them resting on her with a burning intensity that made her feel oddly uncomfortable. They sat at opposite ends of the sofa while they drank their coffee, and it was only when the tense silence between them had stretched to an unbearable length that she risked a glance at him. He was staring at her with a grim whiteness about his mouth which she had never seen there before, and his eyes had the look of a man who had recently suffered the agonies of hell itself.

'Rick . . .' She paused and shook her head as if to clear her mind and rebuke him gently at the same time. 'Don't look like that!'

'How do you feel?' he demanded in a clipped voice as he took her empty cup from her and placed it alongside his own on the low table.

'Foolish,' she laughed in an effort to ease the tension between them, but his expression did not alter. 'Oh, Rick, I'm all right—really I am.'

'Dale, you could have died out there in that treacherous sea, do you know that?' he demanded in that same raw, unfamiliar voice she had heard on the beach, and that strange whiteness about his mouth deepened.

'I know,' she admitted, shivering involuntarily at the memory of those frightening moments, then she met his dark glance warily. 'Are you angry with me?'

'Angry?' the word seemed to explode from him, and then he was beside her, his strong arms crushing her against his hard chest as he buried his agonised face in her fragrant hair. 'Don't you know yet, my little moonflower, that if something had to happen to you they might as well dig my grave alongside yours?'

'Hush, Rick!' she whispered in a shocked voice, her hands tenderly stroking his dark, crisp hair in an attempt to comfort him when she felt him shudder against her. 'Don't say things like that.'

'It's the truth!' he groaned, raising his head so that she could see the awful torment in his eyes. 'God help me, Dale, but it's the truth!'

Her hands stilled their tender caress as she found herself trapped on the brink of something she dared not allow, but when his lips met hers she forgot everything except the wild, primitive emotions surging through her in response to his deep, hungry kisses. Nothing existed beyond that moment, and her love for him rose within her until it was a living, throbbing thing between them. He caressed her a little roughly, his hands roaming her body almost as if to reassure himself that she was alive, but his touch awakened a sharp stab of desire, and she was beyond resisting when he eased the slim strap of her dress off her shoulder. His hand dipped inside the neckline of her dress, seeking and finding the soft swell of her breast with fingers that probed sensually, and his touch was a fiery delight that made her moan softly against his mouth. His thigh was hard against her own as he urged her into the corner of the sofa with his body, and it was a long time before he regained his control and eased himself away from her sufficiently to let his gaze slide over her flushed face. She felt dazed, and her heart was pounding fiercely as she looked up into his smouldering eyes. She loved him, but she knew she would hate herself tomorrow for what she had allowed today.

'It's time you and I had a serious talk,' said Rick, lifting the strap of her dress on to her shoulder, and getting to his feet.

He moved a few paces away from her, but for one brief moment she had seen something in his eyes that

had stilled the breath in her throat, and she knew instinctively what he was about to say. It was what she wanted, but dared not allow, and she got unsteadily to her feet in a desperate attempt to stop him. 'No, Rick, I don't think we——'

'Sit down and listen to me,' he commanded in that authoritative voice she had never been able to disobey, and very slowly, like someone in a dream, her trembling legs gave way beneath her so that she sank back on to the sofa. Fascinated, yet terribly afraid, she observed his restless stance in front of the window where he was silhouetted against the purple hue of the setting sun. His dark head rested proudly on his strong neck and wide shoulders, and anyone else might have thought he was standing there calmly staring out of the window while deep in thought, but Dale witnessed the agitated clenching and unclenching of his hands on the windowsill. Rick might have been deep in thought, but his thoughts were neither calm, nor tranquil, and in some strange way she knew what he was thinking about. It was as if their minds had become locked together as one, and when he finally turned to face her she experienced the oddest sensation, as if their souls had reached out and touched. It was an incredible, rather frightening experience, but she warned herself to remain calm.

'Dale,' he said, his voice deeper and rougher than usual, and she knew then what it must feel like to stand teetering on the edge of a high building, waiting for the slightest puff of wind to send one plummeting down, 'I want you to marry me.'

Her insides felt the jolt; that sickening lurch that set her nerves quivering like the leaves of the quiver tree when the breeze rustled through it, but there was no joy in hearing him say he wanted to marry her, only that dreadful tug of war between her heart and her mind that left no room for anything else.

'Oh, God!' she thought. 'If only I were someone else. If only I were not the child of a woman like Emily Palmer!'

'I think neither of us is in a fit state to think clearly at the moment,' she heard herself say in a voice that was so cool and calm that she was almost disgusted with herself.

'Dale, I'm serious!'

'No!' Her voice broke in desperation, but she controlled it at once. 'In all this trauma you're forgetting about Melissa.'

'Melissa!' His features hardened with anger. 'That's what I came to tell you this afternoon. Melissa's been nothing but a damned nuisance for longer than I care to remember. She came to see me on Monday evening, and, to get rid of her once and for all, I told her I intended marrying you. That's why she came to see you, and you believed everything she told you, as she must have known you would.'

'I never thought anyone could be so—so——'

'Forget about Melissa,' he said when words failed her, and he stood directly in front of her now with his hands thrust deep into his pockets, making it almost impossible for her to avoid the burning intensity of his probing eyes. 'I'm asking you to marry me, Dale.'

CHAPTER TEN

A BOEING flew low over the building on its way to the airport. It shattered the quiescent silence in the swiftly darkening room, and Dale's hand went out blindly to switch on the table lamp beside her. Her throat ached, and it felt as if she were dying slowly inside with every labouring heartbeat. Rick had asked her to marry him, and although she longed desperately to say 'yes', there was a part of her which knew that her answer could never be anything but 'no'.

'That night of the storm . . .' Her voice sounded husky and quite unlike her own as she spoke of the incident which had hurt her more deeply than anything else. 'You came to my room that night, and afterwards . . . you displayed such contempt for me afterwards.'

'I felt contempt for myself,' Rick corrected harshly. 'You'd been placed in my care, and part of my duty was to protect you from the very thing I was doing.' He sat down beside her, his fingers beneath her chin tipping her face up until their eyes met and clung. 'Do you know how close I came to making love to you that night when you so innocently offered yourself to me?'

Her cheeks grew warm with the memory, but a glimmer of understanding was also beginning to filter through into her tortured mind. 'Was that the reason you found me a job with Alex in such a hurry?'

'Yes,' he smiled twistedly, but the smile did not reach his dark eyes. 'I couldn't trust myself around you any longer, and I knew that if I let you stay I wouldn't be able to keep my hands off you. Knowing

Melissa was also a blessing at the time. She's been nothing but a pain in the neck for more than a year now, but I admit I used her shamelessly as a barrier between us.'

'And now you no longer need that barrier?' she asked in no more than a whisper, but there was a flicker of humour in her deep blue eyes.

'Dale . . .' Her name was a groan on his lips as he rose to his feet and paced the floor with his hands thrust into his pockets. 'I was your guardian, and what I was beginning to feel for you had nothing at all to do with the way a guardian ought to feel about his ward. I wanted you, but I had to wait until we were both free of the legal obligations that bound us, and these past weeks I've been doing nothing but hope you'll begin to see me as a man instead of your guardian. I had no intention of rushing you, but when I went looking for you on the beach and saw Tony carrying you out of the sea . . .' His eyes looked haunted in his grey face. 'Oh, you'll never know what it did to me!'

A profound silence filled the room and lingered on until he paused in front of her with a questioning light in his eyes. He was expecting an answer to his proposal, and knowing that she could not give him the answer he wanted made her feel as if her heart was being torn to shreds.

'I—I don't quite know what to say,' she whispered eventually, but she knew that was not the truth, and she gestured helplessly with her hands.

'Say you'll marry me,' Rick murmured persuasively, taking her hands and drawing her to her feet.

Dale would have given anything at that moment to fling herself into his arms. She wanted to cry out her love for him against his broad chest, but she dared not, and she kept her eyes lowered to the opening of his dark blue shirt where the springy hair curled against his tanned skin.

'I shall need a little time,' she prevaricated in a cowardly manner for which she despised herself.

'Time?' he exploded harshly, framing her face with his strong hands and raising it to his, but she refused to meet his eyes. 'Look at me, Dale.'

It was a command, and she obeyed, but not before she had carefully controlled her expression. She was unprepared, however, for the intensity of his gaze. It probed relentlessly, tearing at the hastily erected shutters until it seemed as if he were delving deep into the recesses of her soul as he had once threatened to do, and the fear of what he might find there made her raise her hands to thrust him away from her, but Rick seemed to anticipate her action. His hard arms trapped her against him, and his mouth came down on to her quivering lips with the swiftness of an eagle swooping down on its prey, stifling her protests.

The savage demand of his kiss sapped her energy, and her struggles ceased, leaving her limp and trembling in his arms. She would have given anything not to respond, but her lips parted beneath his, inviting his intimate invasion of her mouth, and her emotions soared wildly. Instead of trying to push him away from her, she now clung weakly to his wide shoulders as if he were the only solid thing left for her to cling to in this dizzying world of ecstasy from which she had no desire to escape.

His lips trailed fire across her cheek, seeking out that pulsating hollow at the base of her throat, and the sensual warmth of his mouth sent shivers of delight cascading through her. The words 'I love you' hovered perilously on her lips, and in a flash of sanity she realised that this was what Rick was trying to wring from her, but she dared not let it happen.

'Rick ... don't ... please!' she pleaded softly in a voice that sounded hoarse and unfamiliar to her ears.

'Don't tell me you didn't feel anything,' he accused

thickly, the pupils of his eyes dilated to the extent that his eyes were almost black with unmistakable desire as they burned their way into her. 'You want me as much as I want you, and if you deny it, then you will be on your knees tonight begging forgiveness for your lies.'

'Oh, Rick, Rick, *please!*' she begged frantically, then something seemed to snap within her, and she burst into tears.

She was lifted at once and carried towards the sofa where he sat cradling her against him as one would do with a child in need of comfort. 'Don't cry, my little darling. You've just lived through a nasty experience, and here I am behaving like a brute to you!'

'I'm sorry, Rick. I didn't mean to cry,' she sniffed eventually into the white linen handkerchief he had pushed into her hands. 'It's all been so unexpected that I can't think straight.'

For a moment Rick did not speak, and there was a peculiar tightness about his mouth when he tilted her face up to his. 'My patience is wearing rather thin, Dale, but I'll give you whatever time you need.'

'Give me the weekend to think it over,' she pleaded at last. 'That's all the time I'll need.'

'Good,' he said abruptly, then he raised a questioning eyebrow. 'Do you feel up to going out to dinner?'

'I—I'd rather not, if you don't mind,' she stammered miserably. 'I'm not really very hungry.'

'Neither am I,' Rick smiled faintly, brushing a strand of hair away from her face and tucking it gently behind her ear.

She sat there in the comforting circle of his arms, savouring his nearness and the knowledge that he had asked her to marry him, but concern for him swept aside her own misery when she realised that she could not send him away without offering him something to eat.

'I could make us an omelette if you would care to stay a while longer,' she offered tentatively, and for one terrible moment she thought he was going to refuse, then he nodded abruptly.

'I accept your invitation.'

Dale escaped from his arms into the kitchen, and reprimanded herself silently for asking him to stay. She needed time to think; she needed every precious second of this weekend to decide what to do, and here she was slicing a large chunk out of it. Fool! her mind shouted, but her heart was saying something quite different.

She kept herself busy, preparing the omelettes and making fresh coffee while she tried to shut her mind to his proposal, but it hovered over her like a dark cloud from which there was no escape.

Seated opposite Rick at the small table in the corner of the lounge, she sensed that he was making an equal effort to keep the conversation light and impersonal, but when they sat with their coffee in front of them they both knew that they had failed. They were saying one thing, but meaning another, and every time their eyes met she was aware of the frowning query in his glance.

'I'll see you on Monday evening,' Rick said finally when he picked up his jacket and walked towards the door.

'Yes,' she agreed miserably, knowing that the present barrier between them was one that she had put there herself.

His hand was on the doorhandle when he turned abruptly to face her, and there was no time to hide the unhappiness in her shadowed eyes. He saw it and, with an angry exclamation on his lips, he caught her up against him and kissed her hard on her mouth.

'Goodnight, Dale,' he said thickly when he released her, and she leaned weakly against the wall beside the

door when he had gone, her lips still tingling from his kiss, and her heart pounding.

'What am I going to do?' she asked herself moments later while she carried the dishes through to the kitchen and stashed them in the sink. 'What *am* I going to do?'

She was still searching for a solution a half hour later when she had tidied the kitchen and switched off the light. She had lived through a frightening experience that afternoon to face something which was still too incredible to believe. Rick wanted to marry her and—heaven help her—there was nothing she wanted more than that. She wanted to be his wife, and she wanted to have his children, but the risk was far too great to even contemplate. She considered his proposal, weighing the pros and cons over and over until her mind whirled, but there was only one answer she could come up with, and it was not the answer she would have wanted to give Rick.

Dale went to bed that night thinking that she would never sleep, but sheer exhaustion claimed her, and she slept through the long hours of the night without stirring until the sun stole into her room early the following morning.

She stared sleepily at the ceiling, trying to decide how she was going to spend the Sunday, then everything that had happened the previous evening rushed into her mind, and with it came the confusion and the torment.

Sister Teresa would know what she ought to do, she thought absently, and then she sat bolt upright in bed. *Sister Teresa!* Oh, *why* had she not thought of that before!

Having made up her mind, Dale was filled with impatience to get in her car and drive up to Durban, but she knew the routine at St Stephen's too well to do that. Sister Teresa would not be free to see her until

that afternoon, and Dale knew that she would simply have to curb her impatience for the next few hours.

She could barely eat lunch that day, and a salad was all she had before she got into her car to visit the Academy. The drive up to the city did not take more than a half hour and, as luck would have it, Sister Teresa was coming from the direction of the chapel when Dale parked her Golf below the marble steps of the Academy.

Sister Teresa held out both hands in welcome. 'I've been longing to see you, my dear.'

'Where can we talk privately?' Dale asked without preamble, and Sister Teresa took her up the steps and into the building which had been her home for so many years.

In the small visitors' lounge with its sombre furnishings, Sister Teresa seated herself on an upright wooden chair while Dale remained standing in front of her with her hands clasped tightly together.

'You look troubled, child.'

'Sister Teresa, I don't know what to do, and you're the only one I can talk to,' Dale whispered, biting her lip as she went down on her knees and buried her face in the nun's lap as she had done so many times in the past when something had upset her. 'Rick has asked me to marry him,' she confessed in an anguished voice.

'And you would like to say yes because you love him, but knowing the circumstances of your mother's death makes you feel that you ought to say no,' Sister Teresa remarked with her usual understanding, her hand lightly caressing Dale's hair. 'Is that it, child?'

'Yes,' Dale cried, raising her pale, tortured face to the nun's, and not caring about the tears that slid silently down her cheeks. 'How can I risk inflicting something like that on him, and how can I risk having his children and ... oh, Sister Teresa, I don't think I've ever been quite so miserable in all my life!'

Sister Teresa let her cry for a while before she said calmly, 'I think you're forgetting something which is very important.'

'What's that?' asked Dale, taking a handkerchief out of her skirt pocket and drying her eyes.

'Rick is fully aware of the cause of your mother's death,' Sister Teresa reminded her gently. 'If he's willing to take the risk because he cares for you, then don't you think you could take that risk for the same reason?'

'You're right, of course, but——'

'Have you told him yet about that letter you found?' Sister Teresa interrupted her, and Dale instantly shied away from the thought.

'No, I haven't.'

'I think it's time that you do tell him,' the nun advised firmly.

'I'm afraid,' Dale confessed, looking up into those brown eyes surveying her so calmly.

'My dear child,' Sister Teresa smiled, 'tell him about it, and thrash this matter out with him. Honesty is important now, and only when you've been completely honest with him will you know what answer to give to his proposal of marriage.'

Sister Teresa made it all sound to simple that Dale could almost kick herself. 'I should have thought of that myself, I suppose, but——'

'But you've been too busy grappling with your fears to think rationally,' Sister Teresa finished for her, displaying once again her wonderful understanding.

'Sister Teresa,' Dale whispered brokenly, 'I—I love him so much, and I never want to—to do anything that might hurt him.'

'Perhaps that's the very reason he's never told you the truth about your parents.'

That dreadful cloud hovering over Dale lifted a

fraction. 'Do you honestly think so?'

The nun smiled encouragingly. 'Why else would he have kept up the pretence all this time if it was not to shield you from the hurt such a discovery would inflict?'

Dale felt slightly dazed. Was it possible that Rick cared that much? He had asked her to marry him, but he had not once said that he cared. She did not expect him to say that he loved her, simply that he cared, but what purpose would that serve if he had overlooked the fact that she might one day become like her mother?

She drove away from St Stephen's that Sunday afternoon in a thoughtful but lighter mood. Sister Teresa had been right. In a situation such as this only complete honesty would suffice, and neither she nor Rick had been completely honest with each other in the past. They had left too much unsaid in their concern for each other, and no decision on the future could be reached on that basis.

Dale was a little pale but outwardly composed when she opened her door the Monday evening to find Rick on her doorstep. She had spent all day preparing herself for this moment, and now there was no turning back. The truth was the only key to unlock the door into paradise, or slam it forever in her face.

Rick raised a quizzical eyebrow. 'Are you going to invite me in, or do I spend the evening on your doorstep?'

'I'm sorry,' she said apologetically, opening the door wider for him to come in, and when he would have taken her in his arms, she evaded him with a cool, 'Please sit down, Rick, I have something to tell you.'

'This sounds serious,' he smiled mockingly, taking off his jacket, and waiting for her to sit down before he did the same.

'It *is* serious,' she told him, lacing her hands together nervously. 'It's something I should have confessed to you a long time ago, but I—I was afraid.'

'And now you're no longer afraid?' he smiled faintly, but his narrowed eyes were watchful.

'I'm still afraid, but it has to be said.' The moment she had dreaded had come and, squaring her shoulders, she met his glance bravely. 'Rick, I—I went into your study one day to find some envelopes for your mother, and—and I found a letter which Ivan Palmer had written to you after—after the death of your father.'

Rick sat forward abruptly, his eyes glittering strangely, but he did not insult her by pretending not to know what she was talking about. 'You read it?'

'Yes,' she admitted, lowering her gaze guiltily. 'I know it was wrong of me, but I—I couldn't help myself.'

'You know the truth, then?'

'Yes,' she croaked. 'I know that Emily Palmer was my real mother, and I know that Nigel Murray was my father.'

Rick's mouth tightened ominously. 'Who told you about Nigel?'

'I confided in Alex, and I told her I'd made enquiries as to the identity and whereabouts of my real father. Alex tried to tell me I would be wasting my time, and I realised then that she knew more than she was prepared to say, so I more or less pressured her into telling me what I didn't know.'

'I see,' was all Rick said into the silence that followed her confession, and his unfathomable expression made the tension pile higher inside her.

'Are you angry with me?' she asked him at last, and he got to his feet so abruptly that he almost startled her.

'I'm relieved, actually,' he said in a clipped voice as

he walked towards the window and stared down on to the well-lit promenade. 'I'm glad you know the truth at last, but I fail to see what this has to do with my wanting to marry you.'

A pang of disappointment shot through Dale. She had hoped he would meet her half way, but it appeared that she was wrong. He was leaving it all up to her and, restless to the extreme, she rose jerkily to her feet.

'Rick, are you truly prepared to risk marrying me despite my mother's insanity?' she questioned him bluntly.

'*Insanity?*' he barked, swinging round to face her, and his expression was a mixture of incredulity and anger. 'What the devil are you talking about?'

'Don't pretend any more, Rick,' she sighed irritably. 'I can almost quote that letter verbatim.'

He lessened the distance between them to stand towering over her. 'It seems to me you saw something in that letter that I must have missed, so enlighten me, please.'

'The part I'm referring to said, "Emily, my poor demented young sister, died in the sanatorium shortly after giving birth to her illegitimate child",' Dale quoted stiffly, looking a long way up into his strangely white face. 'Does that ring a bell?'

'Oh no!' he breathed throatily, his hands gripping her rigid shoulders so tightly that she could feel it down the length of her arms. 'Dale, your mother was demented, yes, but not in the way you obviously interpreted it. She was shattered at the discovery that the man she had loved and trusted could have cheated her so badly. She was admitted to the sanatorium because of a nervous disorder after the shock of discovering the truth, and also because it was so close to the time you were to be born, but she died of a virus infection shortly after your birth.'

'A virus infection?' she echoed weakly, a loud roaring in her ears.

'If you don't believe me then I'll take you to the sanatorium in Pietermaritzburg to look up their records,' Rick offered, his voice reaching her ears as if from a distance. 'The doctors said she'd lost the will to live, and when she picked up this bug she simply didn't fight against the infection.'

'A virus infection,' Dale repeated as if in a daze, then something snapped within her and she was laughing a little hysterically, her slim shoulders shaking within his grasp. 'Dear heaven, it was only a virus infection!'

'Have you been thinking all this time that your mother died insane?' he demanded in a harsh, incredulous voice.

'Yes, *yes*, I——' Her laughter turned to tears, and she buried her distorted face in her trembling hands. 'Oh, Rick!'

She was in his arms suddenly with her face pressed into the expensive linen of his white shirt, and she wept unrestrainedly with the intensity of her relief.

'Is this why you couldn't give me an answer the other evening?' Rick asked when her tears began to subside.

'It's the reason for *everything!*' she sniffed into the handkerchief he had pressed into her hand. 'It's the reason why I was so certain that you felt only contempt for me, and it's the reason why I never dared let you discover how I felt about you.'

'Oh, my darling,' he murmured throatily, tightening his arms about her and lowering his cheek on to her hair.

'And then there was Melissa,' she confessed, her voice shaky in her effort to control her tears. 'I thought you were going to marry her, and that you were simply amusing yourself with me in order to

mock the illegitimate offspring of an insane woman because I dared at times to show my feelings perhaps a little too clearly.'

Rick held her for a long time without speaking, then he forced her face out into the open and looked down into her tear-swamped eyes. 'Do you love me, Dale?'

There was such tenderness in his glance that a melting warmth invaded her body, and pride took second place to complete honesty as she whispered, 'I love you so much that I don't even mind if you can never quite feel the same way about me.'

She felt his chest heave against her, and then he was kissing her with a lingering, tender passion that made her melt into the hard curve of his body as she returned his kisses with a joyous freedom she had never felt before. Time stood still for her, and when he finally raised his head she found she was shaking so much that she had to cling to him for support.

Rick smiled down into her luminous eyes which no longer veiled her feelings, then he sobered and drew her down on to the sofa beside him. This was the moment of truth for Rick, she sensed it in the very tautness of his lean, muscled body, and she nestled quietly in his arms with her head on his shoulder when he began to speak.

'There was someone once, and I loved her very much, but she died on the evening we were supposed to become engaged,' he confirmed what Alex had told her, but this was not the moment to tell him what she knew. 'I decided then that I would never lay myself open to that kind of suffering again, and I succeeded admirably for quite a number of years until you came along. I tried to tell myself, at first, that I felt sorry for you, but I knew it wasn't the truth. Every time I looked into your eyes it reminded me of a calm blue lake, and I wanted to lose myself in its mysterious depths. You infuriated me, and you frustrated me, but

most of all you intrigued me.' His hand was in her hair, his fingers against her scalp arousing a pleasant, tingling sensation that shivered along the length of her spine. 'That night of the storm I knew I wanted to shield and protect you for as long as I lived, and I knew then that I could never let you go out of my life entirely.'

'Rick . . .' Dale tried to interrupt him when she saw the tortured expression on his face, but he continued speaking as if he had not heard her.

'My feelings for you were so strong that night, that I——' He broke off abruptly and groaned as he buried his face against her throat. 'God help me, but I realised just in time what I was doing, and what a child you still were. You'd seen so little of life, and I was supposed to protect you, *not* take advantage of you.' He raised his head suddenly and a smile of wry amusement curved his mouth. 'I had every intention of biding my time, and letting you enjoy your freedom for a while before I asked you to marry me, but things didn't quite work out that way.'

She raised her hand and tenderly caressed his lean, hard jaw in a way she had so often yearned to do. 'Sister Teresa always said it never pays to plan ahead, and that one should rather take each day as it comes.'

'Your Sister Teresa is a wise old lady,' Rick agreed, capturing her hand and kissing each finger in turn, then his eyes became haunted. 'When I saw Tony carrying your lifeless body out of the sea, I thought—I thought I'd lost you too!'

'Don't, Rick,' she whispered anxiously. 'Don't think about it again. I was careless, and it won't happen again.'

'Will you marry me and let me take care of you?'

'There are so many beautiful women to choose from that I can't believe you actually want to marry me,'

she prevaricated, hungering for something she could not even explain to herself.

'Melissa once said you were pathetically plain,' Rick murmured with a hint of humour in his eyes, jolting her memory back to that evening she had heard Melissa utter those words, but she remained silent about it as she felt his warm lips against the palm of her hand. 'Pathetic you may have been at that time, and in those circumstances, but you could never be plain even if you tried. You have far too much character for that.'

'Oh, Rick,' she sighed, not quite sure if she ought to believe him.

'To me you're like a cool, calm and refreshing oasis in the desert,' he continued, and there was a tender warmth in his eyes as they held hers captive. 'I love you, my elusive little moonflower, and I'm still waiting for my answer.'

'Rick, I——' A lump rose in her throat, but she swallowed it down hastily. 'I'll be happy believing you care enough to want to marry me, and I want you to know that you don't have to say you love me if you don't really feel that way.'

A strange light entered his eyes. 'Would you marry me believing that I don't love you?'

'I would marry you and hope that in time you could learn to love me a little too,' she replied with quiet honesty.

'You're a truly remarkable young woman.'

'I love you, that's all,' she said simply.

'I think I'm going to enjoy spending the rest of my life proving to you exactly how much I love you.'

Rick's voice was low and vibrant with an emotion Dale had never heard before, and what she saw in his eyes filled her with something close to awe. He had raised the shutters, and for the first time she was seeing directly into his soul.

'You love me—you really do,' she whispered, and the most incredible joy spiralled through her until her face glowed with a happiness which seemed almost too much for her to cope with.

'I love you more than life itself,' he said throatily, and she could no longer doubt him.

'Oh, Rick!' she cried ecstatically, flinging her arms about his neck, and when his mouth shifted over hers she responded with a warmth and passion that left them both shaken when they drew a little apart.

'Shouldn't we—I mean—does your mother know?' she asked haltingly, a new shyness spreading through her.

'That reminds me. Mother is up at Alex's, waiting to hear from me.' He dropped a light kiss on the tip of her small nose. 'May I use your telephone?'

Dale nodded without speaking, for her heart was suddenly hammering much too fast for a sound to pass her lips, and Rick crossed the room with a few quick strides to dial Alex's number.

'Mother?' he said a few moments later, his eyes smiling into Dale's. 'Tell Alex and Joe to put the champagne on ice. Dale has agreed to marry me, and we'll be there in a few minutes.'

'Do I have to face everyone so soon?' she asked nervously, rising to her feet as he replaced the receiver.

'You're not shy, are you?' he teased, circling her waist with his hands and drawing her against him in a display of possessiveness that stirred her senses.

'A little,' she confessed, her colour deepening at the flame of desire that leapt into his eyes. 'It will take time to get used to the idea that we're going to be married.'

'I'm not going to give you much time, my darling,' Rick laughed softly, lowering his head to trail a path of fire across her throat with his lips. 'We're going to be

married in no less than three weeks, and we're going to spend two glorious weeks at the cottage down at Ramsgate.'

'But, Rick,' she protested weakly even though the thought of a honeymoon at 'Little Eden' thrilled her, 'three weeks is much too soon for me to—to even think of——'

'Are you going to make me wait longer than I already have?' he demanded thickly, raising his head to look down into her shy, glowing eyes, and she found herself shaking her head slowly.

'No,' she smiled up at him tremulously, and he caught her up against him with a fierceness that almost succeeded in forcing the air from her lungs.

'My fragrant, elusive moonflower,' he growled against her lips. 'When I finally make you mine I shall never let you go, and you might as well know that now.'

His warm, hard mouth took possession of hers, and as she locked her arms about his strong neck she found the most exquisite joy in the thought that soon she would actually belong somewhere.

It was a long time before either of them could think sanely again, and when she looked up into his dark eyes it was as if their hearts were speaking a silent language of their own. The years of unhappiness melted away into nothing, and for the first time she could think of her mother with pity and compassion instead of that dreadful, shrinking fear in her heart. Emily Palmer had loved once as Dale loved now, and Dale could almost feel her mother's anguish at discovering the truth about the man she had trusted so wholly with her heart as well as her body.

'What are you thinking about, my darling?' Rick interrupted her turbulent thoughts.

'I was thinking about my mother,' she sighed, leaning confidently against him. 'I can understand

now why she'd become demented, and I can only thank God that I've been more fortunate.'

Rick did not reply to that, there was no need to, and he kissed her swiftly before they left her flat to confront the people she had learned to love, and who would soon become the family she had so long been deprived of.

Harlequin Plus

A WORD ABOUT THE AUTHOR

Yvonne Whittal's childhood was spent in Port Elizabeth, on the southern tip of Africa. She recalls dreaming of the day she would be able to travel to unknown countries.

At a very early age she began scribbling stories. Her ambition to be a writer resurfaced after her marriage and the birth of three daughters. She enrolled in a writing course, began submitting short stories to publishers and, with each rejection letter, became all the more determined.

Turning to the task of writing a full-length book, Yvonne was encouraged by a young woman with whom she was working—an avid reader of romance fiction and a helpful critic.

For Yvonne Whittal, there is no greater satisfaction than writing. "The characters become part of my life," she says, "and when I come to the end of each novel, realizing that I now have to part with my manuscript, it is like saying farewell to dear and trusted friends."